VERONICA

Jane Claypool Miner

SCHOLASTIC INC.
New York Toronto London Auckland Sydney

ISBN 0-590-42134-4

12 11 10 9 8 7 6 5 4 3 2   0 1 2 3/9

Printed in the U.S.A.   01

VERONICA

A *SUNFIRE* Book

SUNFIRE

Chapter One

THE party looked just as boring as Veronica feared, and she planned her retreat the minute she entered the room. As the sixteen-year-old daughter of a Navy captain who was stationed in Hawaii, she was expected to attend a lot of adult social gatherings. Since no one really noticed her when she got there, she always found a quiet corner to read in as soon after introductions as she could and still have her mother think her behavior was acceptable.

This party was at the home of Mr. and Mrs. Bennett, their next door neighbors, instead of the usual navy bash. Mr. Bennett taught math at the University of Hawaii, so most of the guests were college teachers, though there were also a lot of Navy officers and their wives. You could tell the men apart because of the uniforms, but all the women wore the same kind of flowered-print dresses and high-heeled sandals.

The wives dressed alike and college professors made as many gloomy predictions about the possibility of war as military men did. Veronica sampled the luscious fruit that was on the buffet table and wandered from group to group, listening to smatterings of conversations.

". . . This is 1941, not 1914. We'll never go to war again."

". . . The Americans won't be allowed to stand by and not take sides. Mark my words, we'll be at war by the end of 1941."

". . . We sent Janie to a mainland school because we want her to be a real American. So many children who grow up in Hawaii never want to leave. And she'll be safer if there's a war."

". . . No sense worrying about the Japanese going to war with us. They've got their hands full fighting in China."

Veronica went back to the buffet and stood admiring the tropical fruits. There were mangoes, pineapples, papayas, and guavas piled high in artistic arrangements. More pineapple chunks were sprinkled like confetti over the barbecued meats. At least the food was good.

Veronica hadn't minded the parties so much when she'd been younger, but they'd been more fun in those days. Now everyone in Hawaii seemed absolutely preoccupied with politics. She'd rather stare at the punch bowl than listen to any more war talk.

Mrs. Rhoades, the wife of an Army captain, joined her and dipped herself some punch as she said, "I just think it's so good of your parents to let you go to that school with all those foreigners."

"All the students at my school are Hawaiians," Veronica answered quickly.

"But you're not Hawaiian," the woman said. "You're American."

"I'm just as Hawaiian as any of my classmates. I was born right here in Honolulu."

Veronica could see her mother listening to the conversation. Her mother expected her to be polite to everyone all the time. She said it was the first duty of a Navy officer's wife or daughter.

"But they're all such a mixture of something," Mrs. Rhoades continued.

Veronica smiled and said as sweetly as she could manage, "Not all. My best friend, Toshi Nakamura, is one hundred percent Japanese, and another good friend of mine is pure Hawaiian. But my boyfriend is probably what most people think of as typical Hawaiian. He's Hawaiian, French, Chinese, and Portugese."

"And they all go to the same high school." Mrs. Rhoades shook her head. "It's so democratic."

"His name is Mike Kokohuilano." Veronica decided to ignore Mrs. Rhoades' insincere enthusiasm and keep talking about Mike. She wondered what he would say if he were here, and what he'd think about being described as her boyfriend. She decided he'd just laugh. Imagining his laughter cheered her up. "Mike's president of my high school student body."

"But I thought you were? Your mother said — "

"I'm president of the senior class," Veronica explained. She wished her mother wouldn't brag about her. It was embarrassing.

"I'd like to visit your high school sometime and take photographs to send to the States. Hawaiians photograph very well because they're such interesting mixtures."

"Most Americans are interesting mixtures," Veronica said. "I'm English and German and part Scottish and Irish. What are you?"

"Veronica," her mother called, and she knew she'd been eavesdropping. She would catch it when she got home. Now Mrs. Stewart walked over and said, "You seem to be having an interesting talk."

"I just think it's so democratic of you to let your daughter go to school in Honolulu instead of on the Navy base."

"Our house is much closer to Honolulu," Annabelle Stewart explained. Veronica knew her mother would never admit how hard they'd quarreled over her choice of high schools.

"You're certainly an interesting family,"

Mrs. Rhoades said. "I understand you're originally from the South."

Veronica drifted toward the edge of the garden where the smell of the flowers muffled the ladies' perfumes. Out here, the party seemed pleasanter because everyone's voice was softer, and also because she could look down at the Pacific Ocean and the magnificent view of Pearl Harbor below. Mr. and Mrs. Bennett's view was of the whole harbor, while their house next door looked down on only a small part of it.

There were more ships than she'd ever seen in the harbor at one time. She tried to count them but quickly gave up. She knew that the rumors of war with Japan were responsible for the fantastic buildup of ships in the last few months, but she hated to think about the possibility of fighting anyone.

A lot of people from the States talked about the Japanese as though they were all terrible and less than human. But it was hard to grow up in Hawaii and believe that. Mr. and Mrs. Nakamura, her friend Toshi's grandparents, had been born in Japan, and while they were kind of old-fashioned, they were very nice. They always smiled and bowed, and though they didn't speak English well, she knew they liked her a lot.

She knew a lot of other people whose families had come from Japan, and she couldn't imagine fighting any of the Japanese Hawaiians she knew. Of course, she couldn't really imagine fighting anyone, and she was kind of glad she was a girl and wouldn't have to.

Those ships down there in Pearl Harbor were mostly warships. Her father said they were there to warn Japan not to invade the East Indies. Others said they were there to protect Hawaii and the Philippines. Whatever the reason, the United States fleet was more or less permanently stationed in Pearl Harbor this year.

She heard voices behind her and turned as Mrs. Bennett, her hostess, said, "Veronica Stewart, meet Seaman First Class Phillip Easterwood. Phillip is our godson and he's stationed on the battleship *Arizona*. I told him I'd find you because you're closer to each other's ages than anyone else in the room. I told him your father was Captain Stewart."

Mrs. Bennett left them staring at each other. Veronica's first thought was that she wished she'd worn her white sharkskin dress. It made her look older and showed off her golden brown tan a lot more than the soft yellow dimity dress she was wearing. Her next thought was that Phillip was the best-looking boy she'd ever seen in her life. She wondered how old he was. Would he think she was old enough to talk with?

She had to smile at herself. One minute she'd been hoping that everyone would think she was a child and ignore her. Now she wanted this handsome young man's undivided attention. He was tall, blond, and slim, with a nice smile and dark blue eyes that seemed very intelligent.

"If I offer to get you some punch, will you promise not to disappear?" he asked. His voice was deep and very assured but she thought he was still in his teens. She nodded her head, and he turned and went quickly to the punch bowl. That gave her a chance to collect her thoughts, and she sneaked a quick look at herself in her compact. She smiled at her reflection, checking to make sure her lipstick was applied correctly. She wished she'd been able to convince her mother to let her wear the bright red lipstick that was in style. Her soft pink color looked babyish.

He was back before she had a chance to put the compact away. She managed a thank you and a polite question about how long he'd been in Hawaii, and hoped he wouldn't notice that she was fiddling with her purse.

"Not very long," he answered. "But I've come to stay."

She laughed at that and asked, "You mean you're going to jump ship when the *Arizona* gets its sailing orders?"

"No, I mean I'll come back as soon as possible. Now that I've found this place, I'm never leaving. What are you doing tomorrow?"

"I don't know."

"Will you spend the day with me? I have a two-day leave. I promised to go to church with Maggie and Bert Bennett, but after that I'm on my own. Meet me — where?"

"I'm not sure I can," Veronica said. Her head was whizzing, partly because talking to Phillip was exciting, and partly because he was moving so quickly.

"Shall I pick you up at home?"

"No," Veronica said. She had a feeling it would be easier to get out of the house if the date was prearranged with a different meeting place.

"Where?" Phillip was almost smiling but his face wore a determined, intense look.

Veronica laughed and shook her head. "Do you always move this fast?"

"Never," Phillip assured her. "I'm not a wolf, if that's what you're thinking. I just want to get to know you a lot better and I haven't got a lot of time. Tomorrow at noon?"

"I'll have to think about it. Let's talk about it later."

"I want to make the date now, before your folks decide to take you home. Noon tomorrow?"

"What would you do if I said no?" Veronica was teasing but he answered the question seriously.

"I'd spend the day sightseeing. Waikiki Beach. The Bishop Museum. Just looking around and thinking about you."

"And you need a tour guide."

"You might say that." Phillip was smiling now and he seemed to have relaxed a little. "Where shall we meet?"

"In the front of the Royal Hawaiian Hotel at twelve," Veronica said. "But I may not be able to get permission."

"Your folks can call the Bennetts," Phillip offered. "They'll tell the truth about me."

"And what's the truth?" Veronica asked.

"That I'm a nice kid. Eighteen years old. Trustworthy."

"Trustworthy but determined."

"It's just that I understand that you've got to go after whatever you want in this world."

"And you want a tour guide tomorrow," Veronica teased. "Why wait till tomorrow? Let me show you Pearl Harbor." She waved her hand toward the harbor below them. "That's the battleship *Arizona* on your left."

"No. That's the *West Virginia*. Mine's in the middle."

There were seven battleships and several smaller destroyers lined up in a row. "From here they look small, don't they?" Phillip said.

"Yes, like the clipper ships that came to the islands first."

"Bet you know a lot about that harbor, don't you?"

Veronica nodded and said in the singsong voice of a tour guide, "Built in 1898 and named Pearl Harbor because Pearl River empties into the ocean. And, of course, Pearl River is called that because of the pearl oysters that live there. Not too many left."

"I think I already know all I want to about Pearl Harbor. Shipboard life isn't all that interesting," Phillip said.

"That's the trouble with Mainlanders," Veronica said. "No stamina. I'll bet you don't know that Pearl Harbor is the home of the great shark queen Kaahupahau and her brother. And when they built the first drydock they put it right over the cavern where she lived. It collapsed immediately."

"No one believes in that stuff in 1941, do they?"

"No. And neither did the engineers who built the drydock. But after the collapse, they built the others in different places and they never had any more trouble. I guess I'm like most Hawaiians — I sort of half believe the old legends."

"You do know a lot about Hawaiian history, don't you?"

"I was born here so I suppose I do know quite a bit." Suddenly she wondered if Phillip would mind that she knew more about Hawaii than he did. Should she play dumb the way most girls would? She decided to keep right on talking. "Hawaiian history isn't boring like other history, you know. It's full of stories that are really fascinating."

"Like how the cannibals ate Captain Cook?"

"Exactly. But that's not what really happened at all. Captain Cook was killed in a fight that was as much his fault as the Hawaiians. They didn't eat him; they kept his bones because they worshipped him."

"We used to have a joke about the Sandwich Islands when I was in school."

"I don't want to hear it," Veronica said quickly. "Bet you don't even know that Cook named Hawaii the Sandwich Islands to honor the Earl of Sandwich."

"That the same earl that invented peanut butter and jelly?"

"That's the one." Any nervousness either of them had felt when they first met was gone now. They laughed and talked like old friends until her mother came out to the garden and said, "Veronica, it's time to go home."

"Mother, I'd like you to meet Seaman First Class Phillip Easterwood."

"How do you do? We must go now, dear."

"Phillip is the godson of the Bennetts," she began. The simplest and most direct approach would be to ask her mother if it would be all right for her to go sightseeing with him tomorrow. She wished that she had any confidence that a simple and direct approach would work with Annabelle Stewart, but she could tell by the way her mother silently tapped her foot and held her head and neck so stiff, that she was annoyed with her. Even if there was a chance that she would be permitted to go tomorrow, now was not the time to risk asking.

Her mother almost ignored Phillip as she

said, "That's nice. Your father is waiting."

Veronica turned to Phillip and raised one shoulder in a shrug that was supposed to explain a million things. He silently mouthed the word, "Tomorrow," and they parted.

Chapter Two

"YOU cannot go anywhere with a boy we hardly know," Annabelle Stewart said.

"You met him yesterday at the Bennetts' party. He's their godson."

"I can't imagine why the Bennetts would invite an enlisted man to a party with Naval officers. Don't they know anything about navy life?"

"He's a very nice boy," Veronica added. "He said you could call the Bennetts and check on him."

"Of course he's a nice boy," her mother answered. "That's not the point."

"There is no point."

"Don't be rude, Veronica. You will get nowhere with impertinence."

"How can you be so old-fashioned?" Veronica asked. "This is 1941, but you act as though I'm supposed to live the way you did thirty years ago in South Carolina."

"Twenty-five years ago," her mother corrected with a frown. "Your tendency to exaggerate when you want to make a point is extremely distasteful. And the world wasn't as different in 1916 as you may think."

Veronica's hope soared like a flame. If she could find some way to get her mother talking about the past, she might win the argument after all. There was nothing Annabelle Stewart liked more than talking about her girlhood days in South Carolina.

"You didn't even have cars then," Veronica said. "The boys used to come to visit you on horses."

"South Carolina gentlemen preferred horses," her mother said. "Automobiles were not quite . . . not quite socially acceptable."

"But you did have dates," Veronica pursued her point. "You told me yourself that the boys started coming to visit when you were fifteen. I'm sixteen."

"The boys who came to call on me were from fine old South Carolina families. I knew their parents and they respected my family position. You're talking about a common sailor."

Her father's newspaper rattled and Veronica and her mother turned toward Captain Stewart. Veronica hoped that he would put the paper down and intercede for her, but he simply took another sip of his morning coffee and turned the page.

"He's waiting for me," Veronica pleaded.

"I promised him." That was not exactly true; she'd promised Phillip she'd try to get permission.

What would happen if her mother didn't give that permission? Would she ever see him again? She remembered the way his mouth turned up at the corners when he almost smiled, and the dark, deep color of his blue eyes. Suddenly, it seemed like the most important thing in the world to persuade her mother. Never to see Phillip again would be dreadful. "Please," she said.

"You'll just have to tell the young man you can't go," Mrs. Stewart said. "Call the Bennetts, and after this, please don't make any plans without consulting us."

"I am consulting you," Veronica said.

"Your taste in friends is most unsuitable. First that Hawaiian boy, and now a common sailor."

"What's wrong with sailors?" Veronica asked. "You married one, didn't you?" She turned toward Captain Stewart. If she could catch her father's eye he might just possibly cancel her mother's decision.

But Captain Stewart simply turned the pages of his Sunday newspaper and ignored the conversation between his wife and daughter. Veronica turned back to her mother, hoping that logic would wear down her mother's resistance. When she'd been smaller, it seemed as though she'd won some of the arguments, but now that she was sixteen, her mother was almost impossible.

Veronica said, "The world has changed. Everyone dates a lot of different boys."

"It's bad enough that your father actually permitted you to go to the junior prom with that Mike Koku —"

"Kokohuilano," Veronica supplied. The old Island surnames rolled easily off her tongue, but her mother claimed she couldn't pronounce any of them.

Veronica felt the memory of a previous bitter battle rise in her throat. It had taken her a week to persuade her mother to let her go to the prom with Mike, and she still felt pain over her discovery that her mother was a snob. She loved her mother, of course, but she was determined not to let her mother's narrow-mindedness rule her life.

"I thought you'd be pleased that I wanted to go out with a Mainlander," Veronica said. "He's from St. Louis and that almost makes him a Southern gentleman, doesn't it?"

"He's a common sailor, Veronica. You will be happier spending your time with people of similar rank."

"Mother, Phillip is only eighteen years old. Where am I going to find an admiral my age?"

"Don't be impertinent. Just call him on the telephone and tell him you cannot meet him."

"I can't," Veronica answered. "He went to church in Honolulu and we're supposed to meet in thirty minutes. I'd better hurry." She turned toward her father and asked,

"Daddy, won't you explain to Mother that I'll be perfectly safe?"

Her father sighed and put down his newspaper, then he shook his head and asked, "Don't you girls think about anything but social activities? If you'd pay a little more attention to world events, you'd know that none of this is very important."

"Mother thinks I shouldn't go out with anyone at all." Veronica complained. "Tell her this isn't 1916, Daddy."

"This may be more like 1916 than you think, Ronnie. It may be that 1941 is entirely too much like 1916. We're going to be in a war that's already started in Europe, before we know what hit us. And war in Europe will probably mean war against Japan because of that pact the Japanese signed with the Germans last year."

It was the first time she'd ever heard her father admit he thought war with Japan was probable. Usually he was too busy talking about how to avoid war to dwell on the possibilities, but he seemed grave today.

"Nonsense," her mother said.

Veronica was surprised at the vehemence of her mother's retort. She seldom contradicted her husband, but she clearly didn't want to hear anything about an impending war. She continued. "If those Europeans want to kill each other, let them. Americans should stay out of it."

"We probably won't be able to much longer," Captain Stewart said. "Do you realize now that Hitler's army has invaded Russia, America is the only major power that isn't embroiled in this thing?"

Veronica wasn't going to let her parents avoid the issue by talking about something as removed as politics. She asked her father again. "I want to go to take a boy I met at the Bennetts' sightseeing today. His name is Phillip Easterwood. Can I go?"

"*May* I go," her mother corrected her grammar.

Veronica shrugged and kept her attention on her father, pleading with her eyes. "I should think if you honestly think there's going to be a war, you'd want me to have a little fun before it begins."

"Veronica!" Her mother sounded genuinely shocked.

"Maybe the girl's right," Captain Stewart said. "You say he's a nice boy?"

"Oh yes. Maggie and Bert Bennett are his godparents."

"You didn't have time to go to the Red Cross meeting yesterday because you had so much homework. Now you plan to spend the day with a boy. It's your duty to attend Red Cross meetings," her mother accused.

"Have you been skipping Red Cross meetings again?" Captain Stewart asked.

"They're so boring," Veronica answered. "All those old ladies."

"Attending Red Cross meetings is part of being a captain's daughter," Annabelle Stewart grumbled.

"What if I promise not to miss another meeting this year?" Veronica asked. "Will you let me go?"

"Red Cross is a duty, not something to be used as a bargaining weapon," her mother said.

But her father was smiling at her, and she knew that he had overruled his wife.

"Thank you, Daddy." Veronica jumped up from the table and kissed her father on the cheek. Then she ran to her room to dress for her date.

As she left, she heard her mother grumbling, "You spoil her, Charles. She can wrap you around her little finger."

Veronica chose her new white shorts and a red and blue Hawaiian-print shirt to wear. She knew her mother would make another fuss about wearing the shorts in public, but all the girls were wearing them this year. Hers had full legs and wide cuffs that belled out, almost like a little skirt, and she loved the way they looked. She slipped on the shorts and blouse and her new wedgie shoes with the ankle straps, and looked in the mirror critically.

Her soft, reddish-blond hair curled in ringlets around her face, and her warm brown eyes seemed to sparkle even in the dim light of her bedroom. She smiled at herself, picked up her new dark glasses with the lenses that tipped up like pixie boots, and started toward the door.

In order to get out of the house, she'd have

to walk through the lanai, the large wooden deck that encircled half the house. Her mother and father were having another cup of coffee there. Her mother looked up and said sharply, "Go back and dress properly."

"It's just a sightseeing date," Veronica pleaded.

"When you talked your father into buying those shorts, you promised you wouldn't wear them in public. And those shoes! Where did you get them?"

"I bought them with my birthday money."

Her mother frowned and then shrugged. "If you want to wear silly shoes, I suppose I must permit it. But those pants are indecent."

"They're called shorts. All the girls wear them."

"I have told you many times that I have absolutely no interest in what 'all the girls' are doing, Veronica. You are the daughter of Captain Charles Stewart, and we have a position to maintain on this island. Change your clothes."

"Daddy?" Veronica turned to her father.

He shook his head and said, "I must agree with your mother. Those things are indecent."

"Shorts," Veronica said. "They're called shorts."

"That's because they're short of cloth," her father joked. "Sorry, Ronnie, but your mother is right."

"Wear a skirt," Annabelle Stewart commanded.

"Mother, all the girls my age wear slacks."

"Then you'll be the only one who is properly dressed," her mother said.

Veronica dressed quickly the second time, tucking a plain white cotton blouse into her dark blue gathered skirt. If she was late, he might not wait for her. She had to run the last half block to the bus stop, but she caught the bus and arrived two minutes early.

Phillip was waiting for her at the bottom of the steps leading to the Royal Hawaiian Hotel. He looked very pleased and relieved to see her. "I was afraid you wouldn't come," he said. His face was really smiling now — not that half smile she remembered from yesterday, but a look of pure happiness. "You look pretty," he said.

"I feel plain," Veronica confided. "I think tour guides should wear bright Hawaiian colors. Don't you?"

"Plain?" Phillip smiled at the idea and said, "Your colors match mine."

He was wearing a white cotton sailor suit with a navy tie. Yesterday he'd been wearing his dark blues. She remembered that she'd been surprised that his eyes were such a deep blue, almost the color of his dark uniform. Today they looked lighter, almost gray. She decided he was equally handsome in the whites as the blues, but he looked happier today.

While she was looking at him, he was smiling down at her, not seeming to need to talk, but just looking pleased that she was there.

She started to feel awkward about the silence, though, and she repeated her statement. "If I had on a Hawaiian shirt I wouldn't feel plain."

"How could anyone with hair the color of rose gold feel plain?" He reached up and touched her hair lightly, and then pulled his hand back, as though she were a young animal he didn't want to startle. He asked, "Red? Blond? What do you call that color?"

"Strawberry blond," Veronica answered. "At least that's what I've always heard. Lots of people on my mother's side of the family have this color hair. It's Anderson hair."

"What about those cute brown eyes?" Phillip asked.

"Anderson eyes," she assured him. It was fun and a little embarrassing to have him ask these questions. She supposed this was what getting to know someone was like. She'd never dated anyone but boys like Mike, whom she'd known all her life. She tried to look as though she had this sort of conversation with young men all the time, but she was close to bursting into giggles.

"And the freckles?"

"I don't have freckles." The laughter bubbled to the surface.

"Sure you do," he teased. Then he touched the bridge of her nose lightly and said, "Here, and here. Two or three freckles for sure."

She pulled her head back quickly. "I don't have freckles, but if I did, I assure you they would not be Anderson freckles. My mother wouldn't approve."

"I hope your mother approves of me," Phillip said. "Because I expect to be around a lot." He took her hand and said, "We'd better hurry or I won't see anything but the freckles on your nose."

Veronica pulled her hand away almost immediately, explaining, "If someone tells my mother she saw me walking down the street holding hands, I won't get out for a month."

"You mean holding hands with a sailor?" Phillip asked.

Veronica laughed and shook her head. "Just holding hands in public. My mother made me stay in the house once for a week because she caught me eating ice cream on the street."

"You're kidding."

"No joke," Veronica said.

"What's wrong with ice cream?"

"It's eating on the street," Veronica explained. "Not ladylike. My mother wears a hat and white gloves every time she goes downtown."

Phillip said, "Your mother's hat and gloves are probably as natural to her as muumuus and Chinese trousers are to other women."

Veronica looked at the people who were passing them on the street. They were a mixture of races, colors, and languages. Most wore bright-colored casual clothing, but there were others who dressed as her mother did. "I never thought about her clothes as just another kind of costume. You see so many kinds of clothes in Hawaii, I suppose my mother has a right to wear her native costume, too." Veronica laughed lightly at the idea and admitted, "I've always thought of the other women as looking natural, while she looked out of place."

"Hawaii is probably the hardest place in the world to look out of place. I even feel normal in this monkey suit."

"It looks very natural. I have a hard time imagining you in civilian clothes."

"I'm the tweedy type," Phillip assured her. "You'd probably fall head over heels in love with me in civilian clothes. Tweed jackets, baggy pants, and a pipe. Typical college professor."

Veronica laughed and said, "How can you be a college professor type at eighteen? That's silly."

"People are what they are," Phillip answered. "I was born to be a college professor."

"Then why aren't you in college?" she asked him. "Why did you join the Navy?"

"I joined the Navy to see the world. You've read the posters."

"I mean *really*."

"I have a trust fund that my grandmother left me that will pay for my college education, but I can't get any money from it until I'm twenty-one. My folks can't afford to put me through college so I had a choice of trying to work my way through or wait till I got the trust fund money. So I'm killing three years in the Navy."

"Killing years is a funny expression." Veronica shivered even though it was a brilliantly sunny day. "This morning my father said there's going to be a war. I've heard other people talking that way for over a year, but it was the first time he said it. It scared me."

"I sure hope your father's wrong," Phillip said. "I joined the Navy to see the world, not to fight it." Then he laughed and said, "It feels silly to even talk about war on such a beautiful day. Let's just enjoy the sunshine and flowers."

They were walking in the tropical gardens that surrounded the Royal Hawaiian Hotel. He stopped by a hibiscus bush and broke off one of the bright red flowers. "Put this behind your ear," he said. "I always dreamed of coming to Hawaii someday and falling in love with a beautiful girl with a flower behind her ear. Now you'll look just like the girl of my dreams."

Veronica laughed as she took the flower and put it behind her ear. Phillip was right. They were supposed to enjoy life.

Chapter Three

IT was fun showing Phillip Hawaii because he stopped and asked questions, and looked at every flower and tree as though it were precious gold. He was so enthusiastic that after a while, Veronica laughed and said, "You're making me think it would be fun to be a tour guide for real."

"You'd be a good one," Phillip assured her. "You know a lot about Hawaii."

"Probably not any more than you know about Missouri," she said.

He shook his head. "Not much to know about Missouri." Then he pointed to a large rock and said, "Let's sit here."

They were walking in Foster Gardens, right in the center of downtown Honolulu, but it felt as private as if they'd journeyed to some remote island. They sat down on a huge lava boulder and admired the scenery.

"What's that called?" Phillip demanded as he pointed to a tall plant.

"That's a giant bird of paradise. It's the cousin of the small ones over there." She pointed to an informal bed of small birds of paradise.

Phillip looked at the small versions and laughed. "Those plants do look sort of like birds with their bright orange crowns and sharp green beaks. Roosters, I guess."

"Tell me about Missouri," Veronica asked. "Don't you have any palm trees at all? Or flowers?"

"We have flowers but only in the spring and summer. Right now, the leaves have dropped off all the trees. It may snow soon."

Veronica sighed. "It must be hard to be so far from home."

"I miss my family," Phillip said. "Seeing Maggie and Bert made me homesick. But I found you, so that makes everything different. I guess I'm lucky your folks let you go out with me."

Veronica nodded.

"Is it because they don't want you to date? Or because I'm just an ordinary seaman?"

Veronica smiled. "Both, I guess, but I told my mother that I'm too young to date an admiral."

Phillip smiled and took her hand. "Are you always like this?"

"Like what?"

"Cheerful. Fun to be with. Happy."

"I'm mostly happy, sure."

"Veronica," he said. "I was surprised when you told me your name. It seems . . . seems like it would belong to a different kind of girl."

"Veronica Louise Stewart. That's my name."

"Bet you have a nickname."

"My father calls me Ronnie."

Phillip shook his head. "Ronnie is a boy's name. You're too feminine for that. How about Sunny? Does anyone call you Sunny?"

"That sounds like a boy's name, too. Like Junior or something."

"No. Sunny is short for sunshine. I think I'll call you Sunny. You can be my sunshine girl."

Phillip sounded serious under his teasing words. Veronica didn't want the conversation to become more serious than she was comfortable handling, so she asked, "Tell me some more about Missouri. Were you born there?"

"Actually, I was born in Alton, Illinois, but that's just across the river. My mother was at a dinner party and she didn't make it home till a week later."

"Abraham Lincoln was from Illinois." Her conversation was so stiff that it almost made her laugh. But she wanted to stay on safe topics — Phillip's conversation was too intense.

"You really are a history student, aren't you?"

"I'll bet Hawaiian kids get more American

history in school than you do in Missouri."

"Funny your dad being a Navy man and staying in one place all these years."

"It's because he's an expert on Asian culture. He trains people for overseas assignments."

"I'd like to stay in Hawaii."

"I thought you joined the Navy to see the world?"

"Maybe I've found what I was searching for."

"Hawaii?"

"Hawaii and you." He reached out and touched her hair, letting his fingers run through her curls, then pulled her close to him as though he intended to kiss her.

Veronica drew back and shook her head, saying, "You're just a long way from home. You meet someone who's friendly and you think it's special."

Phillip frowned and said, "You make me sound like a foolish kid, Veronica. I'm old enough to know what I want in life."

"Well, I'm not," Veronica said. She slid off the rock and started walking toward the street.

Phillip caught up with her, taking her hand and demanding, "Are you afraid of me?"

"Of course not." Veronica laughed at the idea.

"Don't you like me?"

"I like you," Veronica said. "But you sounded so serious back there and I'm too young to be serious about anyone. I'm still in high school — sixteen years old."

"Juliet was only fourteen when she fell in love with Romeo," he said.

Veronica's laughter pealed out as she said, "And look what it got her! Do you think I want to end up in a tragic love story, Phillip? I just want to live my life and have some fun."

"But the fun of life comes from having someone to love," Phillip said. "The minute I saw you standing in the garden with all those flowers around you, I knew you were right for me. Your hair looked like gold against the blue sky, and then you smiled at me. Do you know how long it's been since someone really smiled at me? Sunny, will you be my girl?"

Veronica shook her head quickly and said, "I like you, Phillip, but I don't want to to be anyone's girl. Besides, you just met me."

"I know what I want."

Veronica tipped her head and looked quizzically at Phillip. She felt pleased and a little frightened by his determination. "Phillip, this is our first date. Give me a chance to get to know you better. Don't try to push me into something I'm not ready for."

He nodded and took her hand. They walked out of the garden and onto the streets of Honolulu. She spent the next hour telling him about Hawaii and showing him the little shops and street vendors that she enjoyed so much. They bought *leis* made of orchids and draped them over each other's shoulders.

Then they found a stand that sold pineapple and hot dogs.

Phillip laughed as he handed her a hot dog. "Back home they'd never believe that hot dogs cost more than a whole pineapple. I wish I had a camera."

"Hot dogs are rare, pineapple isn't," Veronica said.

"Will you take me to see a pineapple plantation someday?" Phillip asked.

"Certainly."

"I can't imagine acres and acres of pineapples growing just like corn in the fields at home."

"I can't imagine acres and acres of corn growing just like pineapples," Veronica teased.

"And next time we'll go swimming," Phillip said.

"I'd better get home," Veronica replied, "or there's not going to be a next time."

She half expected Phillip to protest, but he rose quickly and they found the bus that took them through the main streets of Honolulu and up the hill toward her home. As the bus wound through the crowded streets, Phillip was quiet and Veronica knew he was trying to take in all the sights and sounds around him. But as they left the center of the city and drew closer to her home, he asked, "Sunny, there's no one else, is there?"

Again, Veronica had to fight the impulse to laugh. His questions sounded so formal. She shook her head and said, "Not the way you mean. I date a boy from school sometimes, but it's not serious."

"A high school boy? Your age?"

"He's seventeen. A senior like me."

"But it's not serious?"

"Phillip, I can't seem to convince you of this — I'm not serious about Mike or you or anyone else. I don't think I'm even a very serious person."

"Of course you are. I'm sure you're really a very deep person, Sunny, when you get to know yourself."

They were at the front door of Veronica's house now, and she decided to shelve all of the possible retorts that came to her mind. Later, after she was alone for a while and had time to think, she would be able to sort out her real feelings about Phillip. Right now, her head was whirling with his ideas and opinions.

Phillip came in and met her folks, shaking hands with her mother and saluting her father. He seemed perfectly at ease with them and when he left, Captain Stewart said, "He seemed like a nice boy."

"Too old for Veronica," her mother said.

"He's only a year and a half older than I am," Veronica protested. "There's not that much difference between sixteen and eighteen. Besides, he's only three months older than Mike."

"Mike's a high school boy, and this young man is far from home. Young men who are cut loose from their homes and families can not be relied upon. We know nothing about this boy. At least we know Mike's family."

Veronica and her father both laughed at that. When she'd first started dating Mike, Annabelle's chief objection to him was his family and the fact that his ancestors were from Hawaii, China, Portugal, and France. Now Annabelle Stewart turned toward them, demanding, "What's so funny?"

It was Captain Stewart who managed to point out between gasps of laughter, "You put up quite a fight against Mike because of his family."

"You miss the point entirely," Annabelle Stewart replied. "I don't think either boy is suitable, but I much prefer Mike because he's younger and in his own hometown." Then, she added, "And after all, he is descended from royalty."

This time, when Veronica and her father started laughing, Annabelle picked up her coffee cup and said, "Laugh if you want to, but I'm only trying to protect Veronica from herself. She's young for her age and entirely too lighthearted."

Chapter Four

IT was difficult to concentrate on school-work the next day because she kept thinking about her date with Phillip. During English, she gave a report on the poetry of Edna St. Vincent Millay that she'd been working on for weeks. Before meeting Phillip, she would have been very nervous about it, but today it didn't seem so important.

Mrs. Wilson said she did a good job, but Veronica felt as though she'd missed explaining what she'd really wanted to say almost entirely.

She walked home from school with her best friend, Toshi Nakamura, and tried to tell her what she'd really wanted to say in the English report.

Toshi listened quietly, nodding her head as Veronica went over the report again. Then

Toshi smiled and asked, "How is what you've told me different from what you said this morning?"

"I just don't think I got across to them how her poetry makes the world seem so bright. Even little things are important. Reading Edna St. Vincent Millay makes me feel the way falling in love is supposed to make you feel."

"You told them that small things took on larger significance. I think you did fine this morning, Veronica. You worry too much."

Veronica laughed. "You're the one who worries too much. I probably don't worry enough. At least I know my folks would like me to be more conscientious. About once a week my mother hints that I could get straight A's the way you do if I just worked as hard."

Toshi's smile crinkled the corners of her eyes. Since she was usually quite serious, the smile seemed to fly onto her face and visit a little while, then disappear. As usual, her response was thoughtful. "I think your parents are right. You could make straight A's with a bit more effort."

"Et tu Brutus?"

"That's what I mean," Toshi said. "Not many students respond with a quote in Latin from Shakespeare."

"Everyone in our class knows that line. It's from last year's play."

"They know it but they don't speak it."

"I'll never forget the way Kenny Chu staggered around that stage, moaning and beating his breast. He was a great Caesar, wasn't he? How do you think Mrs. Wilson guessed that?"

"You're changing the subject," Toshi teased. "The point is that you are a scholar in disguise."

"I make good enough grades to get into college. As long as I do that, what does it matter?"

"I suppose it doesn't," Toshi capitulated easily. "I work hard because I need a scholarship to go to U.C.L.A. You don't need a scholarship."

"That's one of the good things about being a Navy brat," Veronica said. "The Navy will pay my way if my grades are good enough. Next year will be fun, won't it?"

"I hope we can fly to California," Toshi said. "It must be wonderful to fly."

"But if we fly, what about our shipboard romances?" Veronica teased. Ever since they'd met in the seventh grade, they'd dreamed of going to the Mainland for college. They had it all planned by the end of their freshman year, and the plans included sharing a dorm room at U.C.L.A. and wonderful shipboard romances with college boys who were also on their way to U.C.L.A. Veronica dreamed of meeting an important football player, while Toshi claimed she would meet an actor.

"Flying's the modern way," Toshi said. "My cousin Harold is getting his degree in aeronautical sciences. He says the day is coming when more people will fly to Hawaii than come by boat."

"I don't think that's possible," Veronica said. "I can't imagine tourists wanting to land on an airfield instead of docking at the harbor. They'd miss the Aloha Tower, the hula dances, and the flower leis."

"My mother probably won't let me fly, anyway," Toshi said. "She'll probably say I'm too young to risk my life. It doesn't impress her at all that planes fly here once a week without any trouble. As far as she's concerned, it's dangerous."

"That's the trouble with being sixteen," Veronica said. "Everyone is so sure who you are and what you're like. My mother thinks I'm a silly little girl and Phillip, the boy who took me to the park yesterday, acted like he thought I was a grown-up woman."

"Who's Phillip?"

"I was waiting for a chance to tell you. Can you stay a few minutes?"

"A few," Toshi said. They were at the gate of Veronica's house now, and they walked into the small garden that led to the lanai. Sitting on the edge of the lanai, Veronica said, "I met him at a party my folks took me to. He's a sailor on the *Arizona*. I took him sightseeing yesterday."

"Your mother permitted it?"

By the sound of her friend's voice, Veronica knew that Toshi would never have been allowed to do such a thing. Though she often felt her parents were too strict, compared to Toshi's they were very modern. "I got my father to say yes," Veronica said.

"And was Phillip nice?" Toshi asked.

"Very nice," Veronica answered. "He seemed to like me a lot. Paid me a lot of compliments and was sort of romantic."

"He sounds too grown-up for you," Toshi said.

"Not really," Veronica said. "It was just a little bit confusing because he treated me as though I was older than I am. I'm used to boys like Mike who don't try to make anything special out of going to a dance or something. And, you know, Hawaiian people are easier to be with."

Toshi nodded her head in quick agreement. Mainlanders always seemed a little more worried, a little more rushed, even when they were on vacation.

"It was just odd," Veronica mused. "I had to fight my mother to get out the front door. She acts as though she thinks I'm growing younger every day. Then this boy — *man*, I guess — treated me as though he thought I was already all grown-up."

"What about you?" Toshi asked. "How old do you feel?"

"I think I'm somewhere in the middle," Veronica said. "It was fun having Phillip treat me like that — I guess it was romantic — but I felt nervous most of the time. It's easier to go to the movies with Mike and hold hands on the way home. In fact, I went out about six times with Mike before he even held my hand."

"Mike's a nice boy," Toshi said. "But not exactly Clark Gable."

"He's very handsome," Veronica said quickly.

"Oh, very," Toshi agreed. "I didn't mean anything bad. Just that he's so friendly and happy all the time. It's hard to think of him as being like Clark Gable."

"You're the one in love with Clark Gable, not me."

"Are you in love with Mike Kokohuilano?"

Veronica shook her head, laughing at the idea.

"Are you in love with Phillip — what's his last name?"

"Easterwood."

"Funny name," Toshi said. "Is it common on the Mainland?"

"No, I don't think so," Veronica said. "But it's probably more common than Kokohuilano."

"Or Nakamura," Toshi added. "It's going to be strange next year. I mean, to be in California where all the people look the same, isn't it?"

"Californians don't all look the same," Veronica said. "Some of them come from

Mexico and others come from Japan or China. You sound like one of those Mainlanders who expect all Hawaiians to be able to do the hula or play the ukulele."

"It won't be like Hawaii, though. I wonder if I'll be homesick."

"Everyone who leaves is homesick," Veronica said. "But I'm not going to worry about that today. This is November and next September is a long way away."

"It's less than a year. It will go fast," Toshi said. Then she stood up and said, "If I'm really going to the Mainland, I'd better get home and study."

Veronica sat on the lanai alone after her friend left, letting her thoughts drift over the last few days. She reviewed the report she gave in class that morning and decided that Toshi might be right, that it probably wasn't so bad. Then her thoughts turned from poetry to Phillip. She wondered what he was doing right now. He hadn't talked much about his life with the Navy, and she decided she would ask him about it when she saw him again.

She didn't doubt that she would see him again. Phillip liked her a lot, she was sure of that. What she wasn't sure about was how she felt about him. Was Phillip someone important in her future, or just an experience that would pass through her life quickly?

But then she shook her head and laughed at herself. She already knew too much about her future. She would finish high school and go to California to college. While she was there, she'd probably meet some nice boy and marry him. But even if she did fall in love, she'd probably come back to Hawaii and teach school.

Chapter Five

ON Tuesday afternoon, Mike asked Veronica if he could walk her home from school. She managed to conceal her surprise and said, "Toshi walks with me, too."

Mike nodded and said, "But we can talk after she goes home."

"Talk?" The word sounded ominous only because any conversation that was important enough to be postponed might be troublesome. Besides, Mike was always laughing, and today he seemed very serious. Veronica wasn't sure she wanted to wait. "What are we going to talk about?" Veronica demanded.

"About us," Mike answered. His face was handsome, with broad cheekbones and a wide mouth that was usually open in a smile. Because his smile was so brilliant, Veronica seldom looked beyond that. Today she noticed other things. His nose was very straight and his eyelashes were so thick and dark that they almost totally distracted attention from his eyes. She'd never really noticed his eyes weren't just brown. "You have green flecks in your eyes," she said.

"My eyes are brown," he protested.

"Not really," Veronica said. "You've got the same kind of eyes I have, only darker. My eyes are brown and gold. Yours are brown and green."

"Maybe we should both get more sleep," Mike said, and then he laughed.

Mike's laugh always reminded her of ocean sounds because it seemed to come in waves that crashed one on top of the other. She relaxed and let herself enjoy the music of his laugh; now she knew that whatever Mike had to say wouldn't be bad news. Until then, she'd feared he was going to tell her that he'd decided to go steady with Lana Achun or some other pretty cheerleader. As president of the student body and one of the most popular boys in school, Mike had his choice of girls. Now that she knew she was still his choice, she relaxed and was prepared to enjoy his company.

Toshi hurried down the steps, carrying a large wire cage with two ducks in it. As she descended the steps, the cage clanked against her legs, twisting her printed cotton skirt. When she approached them, she began apologizing for being late, then set the cage on the ground and said, "These ducks are my science experiment today, but they'll be dinner on Thursday."

"You're supposed to have turkey on Thanksgiving," Mike said in a soft, joking voice. "On account of the Pilgrims."

Toshi smiled and shook her head. "It took my parents ten years to persuade my grandparents to celebrate Thanksgiving at all. My grandparents think duck is better than chicken, and they think turkey is just a big chicken."

"So do I," Veronica said. "I'd rather eat duck, myself."

"Not me," Mike said as he took the cage from Toshi and they started walking down the street. "My mom does the whole thing: pumpkin pie, turkey, and cranberries. I like all that haole food."

The girls smiled softly at Mike's use of the Hawaiian word *haole*. Like most Hawaiians who were completely or partially descended from the original owners of the Hawaiian Islands, Mike was very proud of his ancestors and history. Since he bore the last name of one of the last Hawaiian kings and could claim to be almost half Hawaiian, he liked to remind people of his heritage.

They talked of the usual things on the walk home from school: homework, football, and their friends. As they neared her house, Veronica's thoughts swerved back to Thanksgiving. "Where did your mother learn to make pumpkin pies?" Veronica asked. Mike's mother was part Hawaiian, part Chinese, and part French. His father was three quarters Hawaiian, but one grandfather had been a Portuguese sea captain.

"Cookbooks and women's magazines, I guess. Did you know that, until I was twelve years old, I thought pumpkin grew in cans?"

"I'm still not sure I believe in snow," Veronica said. "Can you honestly imagine what the world would look like if it were all white and cold?" She pointed to a clump of palm trees in front of her home. "Imagine if they lost their leaves in the winter? And the cold. It must be like living in a refrigerator.

"You never get used to it if you're from Hawaii," Veronica said. "That's the reason I want to go to U.C.L.A. instead of an eastern school. When Laura Brown's sister went to Wellesley, she got sick and nearly failed all her classes. She couldn't get warm. Finally, her father sent her the money for a fur jacket and she wore it inside the classroom."

"Maybe it's hard to get used to anything that is different from the place where you were born," Toshi said. "Maybe if Laura's sister was from Massachusetts and she came to the University of Hawaii to study, she would be unhappy, too."

"Maybe." Veronica was thinking of her mother. Annabelle had never really been happy in Hawaii. Then she thought of Phillip and his eager decision to move here and never leave. He'd grown up in a very different kind of place, but seemed to feel immediately at home.

Thinking of Phillip made her feel that her conversation with Toshi and Mike had been very young and kind of silly. Phillip was so serious and so intense and made her feel very grown-up.

When Toshi took back the duck cage and walked down the street toward her own home, Veronica watched her with a dreamy sort of detachment. Toshi was small so she really had to wrestle with the duck cage to keep it from twisting her skirt totally awry. From behind, she looked so young that Veronica was torn between a smile and tears. Toshi would grow older very quickly, and so would she. Somehow, the idea frightened her.

"Penny for your thoughts," Mike said. He picked a hibiscus flower from the bush by their front lanai and handed it to her.

She took the flower and stroked the petals in an absentminded way. This one was a brilliant peachy-pink color. The one Phillip gave her had been a deep red. "I was thinking that Thanksgiving is coming, then Christmas. Our senior year will be over before we know it. Know how older people always talk about how fast the time goes? Well, just for a minute, when I was watching Toshi walk away, I knew what they meant. And it made me sad."

Mike laughed. His laugh seemed to gather strength as it moved through his body and was released into the air. The sound tumbled out and seemed to float around them, mixing with the other sounds of birds and distant traffic.

"What did you want to talk to me about?" Veronica asked. Mike's laughter annoyed her. Why did he laugh when she'd just shared a solemn moment with him? If it had been Phillip . . . but Mike wasn't Phillip. Mike was just a high school boy she'd gone to a few movies with. Mike was very young.

"I wanted to talk to you about time, I guess. I was thinking something like what you were saying. That we only have a little time and then we'll be grown-up. Gone from here, maybe, I don't know. I guess you'll really want to go to U.C.L.A. but I think the University of Hawaii is probably just as good."

Veronica smiled at the thought. There was no comparison, but Mike was like a lot of Islanders who'd never understand why anyone would want anything better than the Island could offer.

"So I thought we should decide to be together now. I mean, we could sort of decide to decide now. You don't have to tell your mother yet if you don't want to." Mike laughed again as he said, "I think your mother will have to get used to me gradually. But we could decide and when we graduate, we could get engaged."

Veronica's only reaction was amazement. She finally stammered, "But you've never even kissed me."

"I just always figured we had lots of time," Mike said. "Then I got to thinking that maybe we didn't have as much time as I thought. I mean, if there's a war, our lives will speed up, Ronnie. So I thought . . . I thought we ought to decide."

"When did you decide all this?" Veronica asked.

"In second grade," Mike said. He was smiling again and leaning toward her as though he intended to kiss her. "I was a slow starter, I guess because I didn't really notice you in kindergarten, and in first grade I was having so much trouble learning to read."

"You make everything a joke," Veronica said. "I don't know when you're serious and when you're not."

"I'm serious," Mike answered and pulled her close to him. She was surprised how much taller Mike was than she had expected. She noticed that he had to bend his head to kiss her, and then she noticed that his lips felt firmer, less tentative than she would have guessed.

She let him kiss her, partly because she felt as though Mike should be the person to give her her first kiss. She tried to enjoy the kiss and feel the excitement that she had read should come from the experience, but when she finally pulled away from him, her emotions were numb and all she really felt was surprise.

"You never said anything . . ." Veronica accused. "I had a crush on you in seventh

48

grade, but you never even seemed to notice me until last spring when you asked me to the junior prom."

"So will you?"

"Will what?"

"Will be my girl. Will decide to decide. Will get engaged to me when we graduate. What do you think I've been asking you?" The question rushed out.

"I'm too young," Veronica answered. And then it was her turn to laugh out loud.

"What's funny?" Mike demanded.

"Just that I'm too young," Veronica said. "I want to date other boys. I want to go to college. I don't want to be rushed. I don't understand why everyone is suddenly so serious about these things. Sixteen is young, Mike. Too young."

He was smiling but she could tell that he was disappointed by her answer. Impulsively, she reached up and put her hand on his arm. "I like you, Mike. I've always thought of you as the nicest boy in school. It's nothing against you. . . ."

"I'm a boy, and that sailor is a man. Is that what you're trying to tell me?"

"No. I told him the same thing." Veronica knew she shouldn't be surprised that Mike knew about Phillip. Honolulu was a small town.

"He wants you to be his girl, too?"

Veronica could hear the hurt in Mike's voice now, and she hurt for him as she said, "That's what he thinks right now. But you know what I think? I think it's too early and we're too young. I just want to have a good time this year and think about all those serious things later on. All right?"

"That means you're going to go out with him again, doesn't it?"

"If he asks me."

"Does that mean you don't want to go out with me?"

"No. I want to go out with you if you ask me. But I'm not ready to be serious."

Mike nodded his head and said, "Okay. Forget I was ever serious. But you know I'll bring the subject up again some day. Right?"

Veronica kissed Mike on the cheek and then she hugged him. "I just want you to know that there's no one I'd rather have give me my first kiss."

"Sounds like you're planning on collecting them from a lot more places," Mike grumbled. Then he seemed to shift moods and smiled widely as he asked, "Do you think your mother would let you go to a real Hawaiian luau?"

"Of course. When?"

"Saturday night after Thanksgiving," Mike said. "My uncle Tu is having a big party for his first grandson. He's one year old — not my Uncle Tu — my nephew. My uncle told me to bring my girl."

"I'd love to be your date, but I'm not really your girl."

"Not yet," Mike agreed. "But you will be."

Veronica hoped that Mike couldn't tell how

happily she'd accepted the invitation. If he was taking her out on Saturday night, then she'd be free to invite Phillip to Thanksgiving dinner. Dating two boys was exciting, but it was also going to require a certain amount of planning and tact.

Chapter Six

PHILLIP wasn't able to get away from the base for Thanksgiving dinner, but he did come by at noon on Friday to take Veronica for a drive. The pleasant holiday that the Stewarts had celebrated together seemed to have put her mother in a sentimental mood, and when Phillip came in, Annabelle insisted he eat a lunch of leftovers before they went anywhere.

Though her mother clearly objected to her dating Phillip, she seemed to like him. She talked a lot about how hard it was to be so far from home and how his mother must miss him. She piled food on his plate and talked of her girlhood days in South Carolina. Veronica wondered what was behind her mother's softer mood and decided it was probably all the talk of war that seemed to hover over the islands like a black cloud.

She obviously enjoyed watching Phillip eat, and persuaded him to have two pieces of pie after a huge meal of turkey and trimmings.

Finally, he pushed away from the table and said, "This is a real Thanksgiving celebration. I don't think I ever ate this much in my life. And it's just as good as in the States."

"You act surprised," Veronica said. "What did you expect when I invited you here? Poi and pineapple?"

"No, but I didn't really expect pumpkin pie either."

"I have a friend who thought pumpkin grew in cans till he was twelve years old," Veronica said. She felt a slight uneasiness, as though she'd been disloyal to Mike for telling that story. But Mike was always the first to laugh at himself so he wouldn't mind.

"We do the best we can," Annabelle said with obvious pride. "I made a special effort to raise Veronica with all the traditions of the Mainland."

"Wait till you see what we do at Christmas," Veronica said. "We have more turkey with all the trimmings, and lots of glass ornaments from Germany."

"You hang the ornaments on a palm tree?" Phillip asked.

"Silly! We have a whole shipload of Christmas trees from the Mainland."

"Have some more pie," Annabelle offered, "You're so thin. I'm sure your mother will think the Navy isn't feeding you very well."

"My mother thinks the Navy's food is great. My mother and father took their vacation in California so they could say good-bye. She had lunch on board ship and we had steak and apple pie and ice cream that day. Not as good as this, Mrs. Stewart, but very good."

"I suppose your mother misses you very much. You're so young."

"I write often — once a week at least."

"And you're an only child?"

"Yes."

"So is Veronica." Mrs. Stewart sighed and said, "I think only children have some special problems, don't you? Veronica is very young for her age."

"Mother!"

"Oh, I know I'm not supposed to say that, but I believe it is true just the same. Don't you think you're young for your age, Mr. Easterwood?"

"On the contrary," Phillip said. "I think only children have the opportunity to be around adults more, and mature faster."

"Perhaps in your case," Mrs. Stewart murmured, and Veronica groaned inwardly. If she knew her mother, she would use Phillip's assertion of maturity as a reason to object to Veronica dating him.

"We'd better be going," Veronica said. Better to get out of there before Phillip stumbled into telling Mrs. Stewart anything else she could use as ammunition.

"Yes," Phillip agreed. "I've got to get the

Bennetts' car back by six-thirty, and it's already two. Do you think we'll have time to get to Diamond Head and back?"

"Sure," Veronica said.

"Please don't use that word, Veronica Louise," her mother said. "Ladies say certainly, not sure."

"Okay," Veronica teased. Her mother hated that expression more than any. Then she kissed her mother on the cheek and said, "I'll be back by six. Don't worry."

Once inside the 1935 Ford that Phillip borrowed, he turned the ignition, then pulled out the choke and eased it in slowly. The car chugged, puffed, and then started forward, only to stop. Phillip frowned and repeated the process, this time pushing the choke in so slowly that Veronica almost laughed. When they were finally on their way, she said, "This is quite a car. I thought you'd never get it started."

"Trick is never to panic," Phillip said. "There's a narrow margin for error in these old chokes. If you give the engine too much gas, it floods and you're stopped for at least thirty minutes. If you don't give it enough, you never start. You drive?"

"Yes, but only my dad's new Mercury. It's a lot smoother than this."

Phillip nodded. "You need to learn to drive older cars, too. Unless you're planning to marry a rich man who buys you the latest model every year."

"I'm not planning to marry anyone for

quite a while." Then she offered, "Would you like me to drive this car? So you could see more?"

"Sure . . . I mean, certainly," Phillip corrected himself.

"My mother has all these old-fashioned ideas about grammar and manners," Veronica said. "Everyone I know says sure and okay."

"Everyone except me," Phillip said. "I'm not going to lose you on a technicality."

He pulled over to the side of the road and they switched places. Once behind the wheel, Veronica was sorry she'd asked to drive. She said, "I've really only driven my dad's car a few times. My mother doesn't drive at all. She doesn't think it's ladylike." Then she laughed and said, "My mother and I are both in the Red Cross and I wanted to join the ambulance corps, but they wouldn't let me because I'm not twenty-one. My mother wanted to join, but when they found out she couldn't drive, they put her in charge of the emergency blood bank."

"Hawaii is really ready for a war, isn't it?"

"We've heard a lot about war this last year but I don't think we really expect it. My mother thinks it's our duty to belong to the Red Cross because my dad is a Navy captain. I took first aid and that was interesting, but the regular meetings are pretty boring. We roll bandages and talk. If they'd let me drive an ambulance, I'd be more interested."

"You look like your mother, but you're more like your father, aren't you?"

Veronica laughed. "You mean I'm not very ladylike? I suppose so. I just think there are so many wonderful things to see and do that it's a shame to let ideas like what's ladylike and what isn't limit you."

"I'm glad you're unlimited," Phillip said. "This way I get to really see the scenery."

They were climbing up the hill now and Veronica needed all her concentration to keep the car chugging up the curving road. She knew the rolling landscape very well and was glad that Phillip could enjoy the magnificent views. She pointed out famous landmarks such as Diamond Head Lighthouse, but mostly she just silently let him enjoy the scenery.

Finally, they were at Leahi Point at the top of the peak. She parked the car and they got out to look down at the sea. "How high are we?" Phillip asked.

"Seven hundred sixty feet," Veronica answered.

They were looking down at the ocean now, and the blues and greens of the water sparkled in the afternoon sun. Soft white clouds moved over the darker, dreamy landscape, making the whole scene look misty. "It's beautiful," Phillip said. Then he laughed and said, "That's a small word to describe it, isn't it?"

"It is beautiful," Veronica said.

"Do you come here often?"

Veronica shook her head. "Mostly when we have visitors from the Mainland. My life is pretty ordinary, Phillip."

"Do you know any pineapple plantation owners?" Phillip asked.

"Most plantation owners live in Paris or San Francisco or someplace like that. The closest I'll ever come to knowing any rich planters is my best friend's father who is an accountant and keeps books for some of the same plantations that his father worked on as a farm laborer."

"That's the Japanese girl."

"Toshi is nisei. She was born in Hawaii and she thinks of herself as American. Her father was born in Japan but he came here when he was two years old. But his father was a Japanese farm laborer. He worked on plantations like those all his life."

"That's one of things that surprised me. How many of the Hawaiian people came from Japan."

"About a third of them," Veronica said. "There are more people of Japanese descent than any other group, including Americans or Hawaiians."

"How did they all get here?"

"The same way nearly everyone except the original Hawaiians and early Americans did. First the pineapple plantation owners brought in Chinese, then Japanese, then Filipinos. They needed cheap labor."

"You really are a good tour guide," he teased. Then he took her hand and said,

"Think I came all the way up here just to look at scenery?"

Veronica knew he was going to kiss her and she was curious how she would feel. Surely his kiss would be more thrilling than Mike's. She turned and let him put his arms around her and pull her close to him. She felt his lips brush hers, then press down firmly, but her reaction to the kiss wasn't a bit stronger than it had been to Mike's.

Rather quickly, she pulled away and said, "Phillip, if we're going to see the crater, we'd better hurry."

"I don't want to see any more pretty scenery. I just want to be with you. Sunny, I love you. You know that, don't you?"

"Phillip, if my mother knew you were getting so serious about me, she wouldn't let me go out with you at all."

"Do you love me?"

"I don't know what the word means. I'm too young to worry about things like that, and I want to go home." Veronica turned and walked toward the car and climbed in on the passenger side of the car.

Phillip followed and said, "Don't be mad, Sunny. I don't want you to be mad at me."

"Then don't try to push me into things I don't feel," Veronica said. "It spoils the fun to have you act so serious."

"I'm a serious person," Phillip said.

"But you said you liked me because I wasn't." Veronica felt she had to make Phillip understand that she really meant it when she said she wasn't ready to be serious. If he couldn't understand that, then she was determined she wouldn't see him anymore.

"I'll give you time," Phillip said. "I won't rush you. I don't want to lose you, Sunny, so I'll give you time. But I don't want you to go out with anyone but me."

"You have no right to tell me who I can go out with," Veronica snapped. "You're not my father."

"No, but I love you so much."

"But I have a right to live my own life," Veronica said. She was surprised at how angry she felt toward Phillip. Wouldn't most girls just be pleased that someone cared that much about them?

Phillip sighed and said, "All right. Go out with anyone you want. Do whatever you want. You're young, Sunny. You need time to learn who you are and what you want."

Veronica stared out the window of the car at the pineapple fields. The mountains in the background were a dark blue-green and she knew that in a few minutes, as the sun went down, they would be purple. Again, she had the feeling that time was moving too quickly. A week ago she had been a schoolgirl whose major worry was whether she would get an A or a B on her poetry report. Now she was a young woman with two boyfriends who claimed to love her. Instead of feeling pleased and flattered to be chosen, Veronica realized she just felt confused and reluctant. She was almost glad to say good-bye to Phillip that evening.

"I won't be able to see you for a week," he said. "I'm on duty every night till next Saturday. See you then?"

"I'm sorry, I promised a friend I'd go to a luau on Saturday night."

"Ask her if I can come along."

Veronica's voice was firm as she said, "It's not a *her*."

"Oh." There was a long silence and then Phillip bent to kiss her good-bye. His kiss was insistent and Veronica did not pull away for a long time. When she did, there was triumph in Phillip's eyes and he said, "You see, you really are my girl, even if you don't know it yet."

Veronica smiled and slipped into her house. If it made Phillip feel better to believe she was falling in love with him, that was all right with her. For all she knew, maybe she was.

But on Saturday night when Mike picked her up, she thought he was the one she might be falling in love with. He looked so handsome and happy in his bright red and white Hawaiian shirt, and he laughed so happily as he slipped the strands of flowers around her neck.

"*Pickake* blossoms," she said. "I love them." They were so perfect and intricate that they were more like carved ivory charms than flowers; they smelled like blossoms from heaven.

That whole evening seemed to be filled with all the wonderful smells and sounds of Hawaii. Once or twice she found herself wishing she had been able to invite Phillip to the luau. He would have marveled at the roast pig turning on the spit, and laughed at Mike's older relatives who danced round and round the barbecuing supper.

Veronica danced with them, doing the simple hulas that she knew and letting Mike's Aunt Rose teach her a more complicated dance that was passed down from one member of Mike's family to the other. Rose was a pleasant woman with a warm, friendly smile that reminded Veronica that she and Mike were related even though they looked nothing alike. Rose's father had been a doctor from New England who died when she was just a baby. She was a kindergarten teacher but her real love was Hawaiian music and dancing.

"I would have gone on the stage if I hadn't been so Mainland looking," she confided to Veronica. It was true that she looked more like a Mainlander than anyone else at the party except Veronica. Though she was part Hawaiian, she was mostly Anglo-Saxon and it showed in her soft brown hair and blue eyes. "I just don't look Hawaiian enough," she lamented.

"Your smile is Hawaiian," Veronica told her.

Rose smiled and returned the compliment.

"So is yours. You're a real girl of the Island, Veronica."

As Mike drove her home from the party, she smiled in the darkness, remembering the compliment that Rose paid her and enjoying the soft night air. They didn't speak until they came to Veronica's street and Mike parked the car in front of her doorstep. Then he asked, "You had a good time?"

"Oh Mike, I never had more fun in my life."

"They liked you, too." He took her hand in his and said, "I'm glad you liked each other. It's important."

Mike's hand felt warm and comfortable but she said, "I have to go now, Mike."

"Yes." He was running his thumb along the top of her hand. It sent shivers up and down her spine.

"My mother will be angry if I sit out in front a long time. My mother has a lot of ideas about how ladies behave."

"Good-night," Mike said. He leaned over and his lips brushed across hers lightly. The touch reminded her of the soft white flowers that hung round her neck. His lips were delicate and soft. She shivered in surprise at her reaction.

"Cold?" Mike asked, and slipped his arm around her shoulders.

"Silly, how could I be cold? It's almost seventy degrees outside."

"That's what Clark Gable always says in

the movies when he puts his arms around the girl."

Veronica laughed and slipped out of the car. Then she leaned her head back in and said, "I really did have a wonderful time."

"I'll walk you to the door," Mike said.

"I can manage."

"I want your mother to know I'm a gentleman," Mike said. He was by her side in a minute and as they walked to the door, the outside light went on — her mother's signal that she'd been outside long enough.

"I'm about to turn back into Cinderella," Veronica said.

"You'll always be a beautiful princess to me," Mike assured her. Then he kissed her again and left her on her front steps. Veronica was watching his car pull away as her father opened the door and asked, "Ronnie? Are you going to stand out there in the dark all night? What are you doing?"

"I was just smelling the flowers, Daddy."

"Well, come on in now. The flowers will be there in the morning."

Chapter Seven

"I know I should be enjoying all this attention," Veronica told Toshi, "but I'm beginning to feel more like the prize in a box of Cracker Jacks than a real live girl."

"Which one do you hope gets the prize?" Toshi asked.

Veronica laughed and shook her head. "You sound just like Phillip and Mike. I'm not sure I want to make up my mind at all. Phillip is more exciting to go out with because he's older and I don't know him as well, but he wants me to stop dating Mike. You know I can't do that."

"If you can't do that, maybe you really like Mike the best," Toshi said.

"I don't know which one I like," Veronica wailed. "It's been two weeks since Thanksgiving and one or the other of them has called me on the telephone every night. My mother is really upset with me. Last night she said she'd like to tell me I can't go out with either boy. Even Daddy said I could only go out on one date this weekend."

"And both boys want you to go out with them?"

"I promised Mike a month ago that I'd go to a party with him. And Phillip really wants me to take me to dinner at the Royal Hawaiian Hotel."

"He took you there last week."

"He wants to go back this week. I hate to have him spend his money, but he says I deserve the best. Phillip's really romantic, you know."

"Just like Clark Gable," Toshi teased.

"Know what? I'm almost in the mood to say no to both of them. Why don't you and I go to the movies Saturday night?"

"My cousin Helen is coming home from U.C.L.A. for Christmas vacation. I'm going to spend the night there. You could come along. She'll tell us all about college."

"They don't have room for me."

"We can sleep on futons. It will be fun. Like a slumber party."

"Helen lives too far out and I'd have to get home for church," Veronica objected. "My father has to go to Maui for some reason. Something about looking for a new training site on a different island. He's leaving Friday afternoon, and he won't be back till Monday. My mother will definitely expect me to go to church with her. She hates to go anywhere alone."

"There's a bus at Schofield Barracks. We can catch the early one and be home in plenty of time."

"All right, I'll do it," Veronica said. She had a funny feeling in her stomach, something between fear and excitement. How would Phillip and Mike take it when she told them she'd be visiting Helen Nakamura on Saturday night?

Phillip called that evening and she told him her plans. He sounded disappointed, but he said, "I guess I'll trade time with my buddy Sam, then. He wants to get married this weekend but he drew duty."

Mike's response to Veronica's plans was, "I guess I don't really have a chance competing with a guy in uniform, do I?"

"Mike, I'm going to visit Helen Nakamura, not going out with Phillip."

"Have fun," Mike said, then he added, "See you tomorow."

Later, Veronica decided that both boys had taken their disappointment about the same way. She confided to Helen and Toshi, "I guess I was hoping that one of them would really get mad and then I could break up with him or something. On the other hand, I didn't want either one to be angry at me. It's complicated."

"Boys are complicated," Helen said, and then, "You took the bus out here with a lot of soldiers. Didn't you see any cute ones? Maybe you could fall in love with someone else and solve your problems."

"Two boyfriends are enough," Veronica answered. "But let's not talk about boys. Toshi and I are dying to hear about U.C.L.A. Is it wonderful?"

"Not exactly wonderful," Helen said quietly. "But I'm learning a lot."

As they talked, Veronica got the feeling that Helen was very unhappy at U.C.L.A. She didn't talk about anything except her classes and what she was learning, but her personality was very different than it used to be. Helen Nakamura had been a cheerleader and a really popular girl in high school, but now she didn't mention any friends at all.

At one point, Veronica asked, "Aren't you home early? This is only December sixth and I thought you only got a two-week vacation for Christmas."

"I took an extra two weeks," Helen answered quietly. "I'm making very good grades so my professors let me leave early."

Again, Veronica had the feeling that Helen wasn't telling them all she could about her Mainland experience. She wondered if Helen had encountered a lot of prejudice in California. It occurred to Veronica that all the talk of war with Japan might make people unfriendly to anyone who was Oriental-looking.

She asked, "Are the people in California nice?"

Helen looked at her for a moment before she replied. Veronica guessed that the look held a lot of things that Helen would never tell. She only said, "Mainlanders are different from Hawaiians. Not as friendly. But they're nice enough in their own way."

They talked until midnight, catching up on all the gossip, and then Helen yawned and said, "I'm still on California time, I think. I'm very sleepy."

"We have to catch the early bus home," Veronica said. "We'd better go to sleep ourselves."

"You can have my bed," Helen offered. "You'll sleep better than on a futon on the floor.

"No, I'm used to them," Veronica answered. "I've slept on one at Toshi's lots of times."

The girls unrolled the soft bedmats and stretched them out of the floor beside Helen's bed. Veronica asked, "Will someone wake us early? I have to catch the eight o'clock bus."

"My mother is up at dawn," Helen answered. "And we're only a mile away from the base." Within minutes they were asleep, and it seemed like no time at all before Mrs. Nakamura knocked gently on the door to waken them.

Mrs. Nakamura gave them tea and rice before they left the house, and then Toshi and Veronica said good-bye to Helen and set off down the road to get to Schofield Barracks before the bus left at eight in the morning.

They walked only a little way before Toshi said, "Look at all those airplanes. There must be a hundred of them."

"They're out early this morning," Veronica agreed. "I guess the war alert is keeping the Air Force on its toes."

"I've never seen planes like those," Toshi said. "And they're flying as though they're coming in for a landing."

"That's silly," Veronica said, "They can't all land at once." She put her hand up to shade her eyes against the early-morning sun. There were a lot of planes in the sky and they did all seem to be coming in together. They circled closer and closer like an angry hive of wasps who were ready to attack. The planes were an olive-drab color and seemed smaller than usual.

Veronica decided they must be from Wheeler Field, which was next door to Schofield Barracks. She wondered how the pilots had liked being called out before dawn on Sunday morning. It was just a few minutes before eight and they seemed to be coming in from some sort of air maneuvers. That meant they'd crawled out of bed very early, and she guessed a lot of them had been out on Saturday night. Things must be getting worse between America and Japan if the military leaders thought such early-morning drills were necessary.

Even for war-alert practice, it seemed strange that so many planes were up in the air all together. In fact, she was surprised there were that many planes stationed at Wheeler Field at all. The planes were getting closer now and the noise seemed louder than she'd ever heard. She guessed that there would be complaints from army families who wanted to sleep late on Sunday morning.

It occurred to her that the planes might not be on manuevers but might have responded to some sort of warning of possible attack. She knew Hawaii had been on war alert for several months, and from time to time there were rumours of impending disaster. Just before Thanksgiving, one of the Hawaiian newspapers ran headlines about an impending invasion and sent everyone scurrying around to buy newspapers but it had come to nothing.

As she watched the planes come closer, fear tightened and coiled in her stomach and her heart began to beat faster. She remembered the story about the little boy who cried wolf too many times. Maybe this was different from all the other alerts. All those planes must mean some kind of trouble!

The planes circled closer now and the noise grew very loud, setting up a sound that seemed to rock the very earth they stood on. She could see the ends of their red wingtips as they dipped to make a turn. She strained her eyes to see what they had painted on the underside of their wings. And there was something larger and red attached to their bodies. These were not Wheeler Field planes at all!

"They've got red things on them." Toshi pointed to the airplanes again.

Both girls knew that the red circles were the Japanese emblem, but Veronica didn't see any sense in telling Toshi how frightened she was. She pointed to the road and said, "There's our bus. We'd better hurry."

The yellow bus sat just inside the entry gate at Schofield. The girls waved at the sentries and walked quickly into the barracks. When they reached the bus, it was empty and the keys hung in the ignition. "Driver's gone for coffee," Veronica said. "We must be early."

"What?" Toshi yelled. The airplanes they'd seen earlier were so close now and there were so many of them that it was impossible to hear anything.

It was the fact that Toshi had to yell to be heard that jarred Veronica into understanding. Those airplanes were getting too close. "They're going to crash!" Veronica yelled. She grabbed Toshi's hand and ran away from the bus toward a small hill where a maintenance shack stood.

It only took a few seconds to reach the top of the little hill. When they got there, they stopped and turned to look at the planes again.

They were so close now that the girls could actually see the pilots' heads sticking out of the planes. They flew in such close formation that it looked as though their wings might touch. Toshi shaded her eyes against the morning sun and strained to see more clearly. She shouted, "They're Japanese planes."

"How could they be?" Veronica shouted back. The roar of the engines was frightening her and she could feel her heart beating at a pace that she couldn't imagine possible.

"The Rising Sun," Toshi yelled back, and then pointed to the planes again.

Veronica knew she was pointing to the bright red spots painted on the wings of the planes and she understood. The Japanese were attacking. "We've got to warn them," she shouted. But she never knew whether or not Toshi heard her because at that moment, the bombs began to fall.

Chapter Eight

THE two girls stood at the top of the hill and watched the bombs fall through the air onto the ground. Veronica was still holding Toshi's hand as though, by holding onto something familiar, she could protect her sanity and understand that what she was watching was really happening.

Her mind was almost as frozen as her body, but somewhere in the back of Veronica's brain, the thought that they might personally be in danger kept trying to push through. But it was a thought without any emotion behind it. She felt no fear, nor did she feel anger as she watched the horror unfolding. All she could do was try to understand the scene. For those first few seconds, the girls were frozen observers who stood upon the hill and watched the attack as though it were a movie.

The Japanese planes flew in close formation until they came in for the kill. As they neared the barracks, they peeled off from the group and dipped lower toward the ground. The wings looked to Veronica as though they might graze the roofs of the buildings they were bombing in a gesture of final insult before dropping their lethal loads.

There was always a few seconds' delay as the bombs dropped down to the earth, then there would be a loud noise, and clouds of heavy black smoke would rise as though from hell. As each bomb hit, Toshi's grip tightened on her hand in fierce spasms. Once, when an ammunitions barrack burst into flames, Veronica thought Toshi might break the bones in her hand.

The planes roared with a huge, angry wave of sound that grew louder and louder as more of them came in for the kill. Along with the warning that they should take cover, another thought was tickling her brain: She had heard that sound before.

The whole scene seemed even more insane because the Hawaiian sky was never more beautiful. Tiny white clouds floated above the terrible scene with perfect serenity. Veronica simply couldn't accept that she was seeing what she was seeing. Her mind sent her a series of silent protests as though it were battling against reality.

"It's Sunday," she thought. "You can't sneak in and bomb us on Sunday. That's not fair." Then she laughed aloud at the idea that war had to be fair. She was the daughter of a military man and she knew that much about war — it wasn't a game with rules; it was a fight to death.

The planes circled round and round, dipping to the ground and unloading bombs, then climbing skyward where they circled. Some of the earliest bombers left, but others came in for another attack. There was not much moving on the ground and, as far as Veronica could see, there wasn't anyone who was trying to resist.

The later planes didn't have quite as easy a time as their earlier comrades did because several men set up machine guns and shot at them from the center of the road. She saw one Japanese plane dive down to drop its bombs, then keep right on diving until it crashed into the ground. The plane went up in a blaze of red fire and Veronica felt that was one enemy less.

She wished she had a machine gun, and knew with all her heart that if she'd had any weapon at all, she would have been down there fighting. The rage she felt was beyond anything she might ever have imagined. It was a boiling black hatred that made her capable of anything. At that moment she knew that she was willing to kill, and if she got the chance, she would.

At the same time she found the depths of her violent anger, she remembered where she had heard a noise like that of the planes. Once, when she was very small, she'd watched a tidal wave hit the beach. She could remember standing on their porch and looking down onto Waikiki beach, watching as the huge wave smashed onto the shore. The sound had come from a long distance but it was a softer version of what she was hearing today.

From their vantage point, Toshi and Veronica could see much of Schofield Barracks. The long, low buildings were spread out along the earth in perfect order.

Toshi turned to her and stared with wide-open eyes that seemed to be asking a million questions. When she saw the fear and shock in Toshi's eyes, she understood that she was almost in shock herself.

Her mind began to function and she began to feel the fear that she'd been repressing. Waves of nausea hit her and almost knocked her over, but she didn't collapse. Instead, she said, "We've got to get down there and see if we can help."

She pointed toward the scene below. Hundreds of people were milling around in shocked confusion now. They looked small and frantic from the top of the hill. They were running around in circles but no one seemed to be doing anything about the fires that blazed all over the barracks field. Every few seconds the sound of ammunition bursting into flames would add to the general bedlam.

The Japanese planes seemed to be leaving now, though several dozen still circled the area. As far as Veronica could see, not one American plane had taken off from Wheeler Field. She knew the whole attack had probably happened very quickly, but she couldn't believe how slowly the Americans were responding. It was easy to see by the way people ran around in circles that things were completely disorganized.

Toshi asked, "Where are our planes?"

A siren shrilled over the sounds of the planes and the shouts of people. Two other sirens joined in, making it almost impossible to talk. "Come on," she shouted to Toshi.

Toshi shook her head, pointing to the sky. Veronica could read the pure terror in her friend's eyes, and she knew from the sound of airplane engines coming closer that they were coming back for another attack. She looked into the sky where Toshi pointed.

It was only one plane and it came full speed toward the ground. Veronica watched in horror as the Japanese plane crashed deliberately into the largest barrack. Flames spewed up and sirens sounded, but the barrack did not explode. Veronica sighed in relief because she was afraid that it might have been filled with ammunition. If it had been, the whole area would have been totally wiped out.

That Japanese pilot had deliberately forfeited his life to destroy his target. If they were all like that, they would be a formidable enemy. Veronica felt fear as well as anger, and most of all she felt the need to act.

Now, smaller explosions crackled intermittently and smoke from the many fires drifted into a layer of darkness over most of Schofield Barracks and Wheeler Field.

The air was full of flames and heavy black smoke. The Japanese planes were almost all gone and the sound of their disappearing engines was peppered by the rat-a-tat-tat of machine guns. Between the sirens and explosions and sounds of motors, Veronica could hear human voices shouting to each other. She could also hear screams of fear and pain from the wounded.

Tears ran down Toshi's cheeks as she asked again, "Where are our planes?"

"Still in the hangars," Veronica yelled back.

"But why didn't they fight back?" Bewilderment, anger, and fear all played across Toshi's usually passive features. She began wringing her hands and asking again and again, "Why don't they fight back? Why don't they fight back?"

Veronica realized that her friend was more shocked and frightened than she was. She was going to have to keep Toshi going as well as herself, at least for a little while. "We must go see if we can help," Veronica said.

"What if they come back?" Toshi asked.

"They're gone now," Veronica said. "They've dropped all their bombs. We must help."

"But what can we do?" Toshi asked. She

was still wringing her hands, but at least she had changed the question she was repeating to, "What can we do now?"

"There are wounded people down there. I've had Red Cross training." Veronica almost laughed again as she said that. What good would her few lessons in first aid do at a time like this? Still, she insisted, "Toshi, let's go."

She had to almost drag Toshi down the hill, but by the time they got to the entrance of the barracks, Toshi seemed more in control of herself. They went to the entrance where the sentries were still standing with their guns pointed at the sky. Just as they got there, three ambulances raced through the door with their sirens going full blast. Veronica realized that they were taking the wounded to the hospital in Honolulu.

For some reason she didn't understand, Veronica looked at her watch then and was dismayed to see that it was only a few minutes after eight. All this destruction had been accomplished so quickly. She could hardly believe that that little time could make such a difference. The scene at Schofield Barracks was totally transformed. Fires blazed out of control. Men were running around shouting at each other in total confusion. She decided that the best thing for them to do was to report to the sentries and ask for orders.

There was only one sentry at the gate, and when they approached him, he pointed his gun at them and asked, "Where do you think you're going?" he demanded.

It was hard to talk over all the noise. She could hear someone screaming over all the other sounds. She hoped he got help quickly because she had never heard the sound of such pain. "I've had first aid and we want to help."

"Get out of here fast," the soldier said. "Get back to town."

Cars were pouring out of the barracks now. Veronica could see that many of the cars held wounded men. She repeated her request. "We want to help."

"Just get away," the soldier shouted. "We've got enough trouble without you kids." He turned his back to them. Veronica spotted an officer just inside the gate. He had on his uniform jacket but he was wearing his pajama bottoms and slippers. He seemed to be trying to restore some order to the traffic jam that was forming at the entrance of the barracks. Several cars and ambulances obviously wanted to get through the entrance at once.

As the girls walked toward the officer, the cars began to blow their horns, adding a shorter, more insistent message to the continual whine of the sirens. It was hard to shout loud enough to be heard. "I've had first aid. How can I help?"

"Get out of here," he said. He pointed to the entrance and then turned back to the cars he was directing. Veronica ran back to the sentries who were standing there. "What can we do?" she asked.

"Evacuate," he shouted. Then he pointed to the bus that they had planned to take into town. It was apparently in line to leave the barracks. On the front was a sign that proclaimed its destination: PEARL HARBOR.

"Evacuate," the sentry repeated.

Veronica grabbed Toshi's hand and said, "Let's go home."

Toshi followed her to the entrance of the bus but wouldn't get on. "I'm going back to my uncle's house," she said.

"But they told us to go home."

"My aunt will be too worried," Toshi said. "And they may be hurt. Maybe they bombed there, too."

Until then, it hadn't occurred to Veronica that the Japanese planes might have bombed anywhere except Schofield Barracks. She was certain they wouldn't bomb the Nakamura house except as a mistake, but she did begin to worry about the other military bases on the island. Was it possible that they'd bombed Hickam Field as well? Or one of the other islands like Maui? A sudden fear for her father's safety stabbed her. He wouldn't be home until tomorrow so there wouldn't really be any way to know if he was all right until then.

The Nakamuras had a telephone so it might be best to do as Toshi wanted and go there first. At least she would be able to phone her mother and say she was all right. Her mother would be very worried about her when she heard about the bombs.

"All right," Veronica said, and they ran around the bus and into the street, turning away from the road the others were taking, and heading toward the Nakamura household.

Once they were on the road, it seemed as though they were leaving a nightmare behind them. The sounds dimmed and then died out. The sky was the usual bright morning blue, but when they paused at the first turn and looked back, they could see that the fires were growing. Black smoke followed them like an ugly dragon that magically transformed the beautiful landscape into a charred desert.

"Let's run," Toshi said. Veronica ran as fast as she could, as though by running there was some way she could run backward in time and erase the dreadful sounds and sights that they'd just seen. As she ran, she kept the picture of the Nakamura home in her mind. She remembered the delicately landscaped garden, and the simple and beautiful feeling of the rooms inside.

Before they were half a mile down the road, they ran into a barricade of three army cars parked across the road. Ten soldiers ran toward them with guns drawn. One asked, "Where are you going?"

"To my uncle's house," Toshi said. They were both panting and out of breath.

"No. Go back," the soldier said. "This road is closed."

"But my uncle lives there."

"Go back," the soldier said and pointed his gun at Toshi.

"But my uncle. . . ."

Veronica saw him put his thumb on the trigger of the gun and sensed the danger they were in. These soldiers were very frightened and possibly so confused that they would think Toshi was the enemy. She said, "We'll go back to Honolulu, Toshi. You can see your uncle later."

"I need to see my uncle," Toshi protested.

Veronica took her hand and pulled her backwards, away from the soldiers. They didn't run back to Schofield Barracks, but they did walk at a fast trot. When they got closer, their steps slowed because they dreaded what they would see there.

The same sentry met them at the gate. This time, he also pointed his gun at them and demanded, "Who goes?"

"We want to go back to Honolulu," Veronica said.

"Evacuate," Toshi added.

"Women and children all evacuated," the soldier said. He seemed dazed and very confused. As they talked, an ambulance drove through the entrance and set off on the road to Honolulu.

"What about the bus?" Veronica asked.

"You missed it," he answered.

"How can we get back to town?" Veronica asked.

"Walk," the soldier said.

"We can't walk," Veronica protested. "Maybe we'd better come back inside. We could help."

The soldier shook his head, stepping forward slightly and pointing the gun at them again. "No Japs allowed," he said.

Veronica took Toshi's hand and they practically ran away from Schofield Barracks toward Honolulu.

"It's fifteen miles," Toshi protested. "It will take hours to get there."

"Maybe someone will give us a ride," Veronica said.

A few cars passed them but they seemed too full of people to offer any real hope of transportation. None slowed down when they waved.

Veronica knew that many of the people who passed them were too frightened to even see them. As she walked, she grew more and more frightened herself. The enormous impact of what they had just seen began to dawn on her. Japanese planes had attacked Schofield Barracks and that would have to mean war.

"What if they come back?" Toshi asked.

"They won't," Veronica answered. Even as she answered, she heard the long, low roar of engines. She turned to look into the sky, following the sound, and sighed with relief when she saw that they were only two large American airplanes — the kind she was accustomed to seeing in the sky.

"Those are ours," Veronica said.

"They'll fight back," Toshi said confidently. "They'll find the planes and shoot them down."

Veronica wondered how much good two planes would do. The Japanese planes had seemed to number in the hundreds.

Chapter Nine

"THAT ambulance has stopped," Veronica said. She pointed to a Red Cross ambulance that was up ahead on the road. "Maybe they'll give us a ride."

The girls ran toward the ambulance, and when they got there, Veronica asked, "Do you have room for us?"

A woman in a bathrobe with her hair in metal curlers was driving. She had a small boy beside her on the front seat. He was screaming at the top of his lungs, as were the three children in the rear of the ambulance.

The boy's head was bleeding and the woman held a blood-soaked cloth to the wound with one hand as she worked to start the car with the other. She had also been cut around the eyes, but her wounds were only superficial and they'd stopped bleeding by themselves.

She looked absolutely frantic as she answered. "Something's wrong with this ambulance. My son is shot and I have to get him to the hospital." Then the woman began sobbing hysterically and turning the ignition of the car, grinding the starter as she pushed on the accelerator.

Veronica smelled gas and said, "It's flooded. "You'll have to wait for a while."

"I can't wait," the woman wailed. "I've got three children, and my boy is dying. And when the Japs come back we'll all be killed." She turned the ignition again and the battery rumbled and coughed.

"If you keep that up you'll run down the battery. Then the ambulance won't go at all." She wondered whether she ought to look at the children in the back first, or offer to help staunch the flow of blood from the boy's wound.

"Do something," the woman demanded. "Make the ambulance run."

Veronica's mind was racing as she reviewed everything she knew about cars. She said, "I think you should try pressing your foot all the way down on the accelerator. Don't pump it, just keep it there."

The child beside her stopped screaming and called out in a clear voice, "Mama, am I going to die?"

"No, of course not," the woman answered. She slid out of the driver's seat and cradled the boy in her arms. Veronica told Toshi to look at the children in the back, and she got in behind the wheel of the ambulance. Though she knew first aid and Toshi didn't, she was also the only one who could drive the ambulance, and the most important thing seemed to be to get the children to the hospital.

The first thing she saw was that the woman had the choke pulled all the way out. She reached out and took hold of the choke, then she said a fast prayer as she pressed her foot down on the accelerator. She held her foot steady as the ambulance coughed, whined, complained, and jumped. Then the engine caught hold.

Gently, ever so gently, Veronica pushed the choke in a millimeter at a time. Then she eased her foot off the accelerator just as gently until it was positioned so it wouldn't send them hurtling off and then stall again. Once she had the choke in and the accelerator pressure correct, she began the most difficult part: letting out the clutch. One false move and the engine would stop, and they'd have to begin all over again. Or worse, yet, the battery wouldn't catch hold and they'd be permanently stuck.

At first the ambulance showed signs of wanting to stall again. It chugged and coughed and bumped along, but Veronica held it steady and she eventually got it up to normal speed. She sighed in relief and said, "I think we'll be in Honolulu in about forty minutes."

"We've got to get there a lot faster than that," the woman said. "My little boy is bleeding."

Veronica could hear that the woman was really struggling not to lose control again. The boy was still screaming but his voice sounded weaker than it had a few minutes earlier. "How did your boy get hurt?" she asked.

"I'm not sure," she answered. "One minute we were asleep, and the next minute there was flying glass exploding in our faces. I ran outside and grabbed the ambulance."

"How did you get it?"

"The keys were in it," she answered.

From her answer, Veronica realized the woman had taken the ambulance without any kind of permission at all. Was it stealing to do something like that in wartime? She decided that people did a lot of things in wartime that wouldn't really be acceptable under normal circumstances. The woman was obviously very concerned about her children and that was only natural. "Hold the cloth directly on the cut," Veronica said. "Use the pressure of your fingers to stop the bleeding."

"Just go as fast as you can," the woman said. "Thank God you came, Veronica."

"You know me?" Veronica asked. She glanced quickly at the woman sitting beside her.

The woman said, "I'm Mary Rhoades."

It took her a while to place the name, and then she figured out that the woman beside her was Mrs. Rhoades, one of the people who'd been at the party at the Bennetts'. She'd said her husband was in the Army.

"The bleeding's getting worse," Mrs. Rhoades said. "You'll have to go faster."

"Keep that cut pulled together as tight as you can," Veronica commanded. She called back to Toshi, "Is anyone else hurt?"

"Not really," Toshi said. "How long before we get there?"

"I'm driving as fast as I can," Veronica said.

"Turn on the siren," Mary Rhoades commanded. "You'll have to go faster."

"I'm driving almost sixty miles an hour," Veronica objected. "I've never driven over thirty-five miles an hour before."

"You have to!" Her command was somewhere between a plea and a shout.

"She's right," Toshi said. "We've got to get help."

Veronica took a deep breath and pulled out the siren knob, then she put her foot all the way down on the accelerator. From that point on, until they pulled into the outskirts of Honolulu and she absolutely had to slow down, she didn't pay any attention to anything except the steering wheel and the road.

She was so intent on the road and getting there that she almost forgot to slow down as they came to the curve in the road that would lead them into the town of Honolulu. But she remembered in time and slowed enough to make the turn sensibly. As they rounded the corner, she looked expectantly toward the town below. Until that moment, it hadn't occurred to her that the Japanese might have attacked Pearl Harbor as well as Schofield Barracks.

Veronica slowed the ambulance to a crawl as they looked down onto the city. They were too far away to see everything, but it was clear that the Japanese planes had wreaked havoc. Smoke rose in black billows and there were several fires. Veronica did her best to keep her voice level as she said, "I'm not sure whether they bombed the town or just the harbor."

Her hands and voice were shaking as she rounded the familiar streets that led toward the city. They were in the part of town that she knew best now. In just a few minutes, they'd be at the corner where you turned off to get to her home. She wanted with all her heart to go home but she felt it was her duty to drive the children straight to the hospital.

Maybe her mother had seen the whole thing from her backyard. Or maybe she'd gone over to the Bennett's where she could really see all of Pearl Harbor. Her breath caught as she thought of Phillip. Was his ship hit? Had he been hurt?

The impact of the destruction she was seeing hit her full force. There would be people she knew whom she'd never see again. Phillip might be hurt or even killed! And Mike — where was he? It was too horrible to think about. She wanted to turned the ambulance around and run in the other direction, but with the wounded children who were in her charge, that was impossible. Whatever else happened, she had to find a way to get them to the hospital. She tried not to think about anything but keeping her attention on the wheel.

They were driving slower now because the traffic was getting heavier and they weren't sure what they would come up against next. None of them talked much, but Mrs. Rhoades did ask in a panicked voice, "What if they bombed the hospital?"

"They wouldn't," Veronica said in horror.

"Wouldn't they?" Mrs. Rhoades asked. "The Japanese are horrible people. You can't trust them. I've always known that. Horrible people."

Veronica hoped that the noise of the ambulance motor and the cries of the children were loud enough so that Toshi couldn't hear what Mrs. Rhoades was saying. It was easy to understand why she hated the Japanese so much, but Toshi was American. Yet it would hurt her to hear the angry ranting.

Silly to worry about someone getting her feelings hurt when they were looking at such absolute destruction. Yet Veronica knew that Toshi and her family would probably feel worse than she could even imagine about the fact that the enemy was Japanese. She thought of old Mr. Nakamura and how proud he was that his children were American citizens. How would he feel about Japan — the country where he was born?

"My God, they're coming back," Mrs. Rhoades screamed. She pointed to the sky above Pearl Harbor. Veronica lifted her eyes to the sky and shuddered at what she saw. There were hundreds of planes flying in from the sea. And the way they flew in an angry, tight formation, told her that they were Japanese bombers coming back for a second attack.

She turned the corner quickly and said, "I live here. We'd better take cover."

"We've got to get to the hospital," Mrs. Rhoades said. In the next breath, she screamed, "They're going to bomb the city! Let's go back to Schofield."

"We've got to find shelter," Veronica answered. "We can't drive into a bombing raid."

"You coward!" the woman screamed. "You're going to kill my children!"

"I'm going to save us all if I can," Veronica answered grimly. She was determined not to let Mrs. Rhoades' hysterical screams influence her decision. The most important thing was to find shelter from this next onslaught. If any of them survived the raid, they could continue the journey. If they drove into that bedlam, they would surely all be killed.

"Get back on the road," Mrs. Rhoades screamed. "I want to take my babies to the hospital."

"We'll get help here," Veronica said. She pulled into her driveway and ran to the door. The house was locked, and she knew that her mother had found some way to get to her emergency Red Cross post. And the cook wasn't in because it was Sunday morning. Veronica realized that she'd lost her purse with her key sometime in the last half hour.

Though she knew she could probably find a window that was open, she decided to take everyone to the Bennetts' house instead. It would be easier and they could watch the city better from there. Mrs. Bennett had the best view.

It only took a minute for Mrs. Bennett to open the door, and she smiled in a surprised manner. "Veronica, dear, what a pleasant surprise."

"Mrs. Bennett, can we stay here? We need your help. Will you help me get the children out of the ambulance before they come back?"

"What on earth are you talking about?"

"Help me. We've got to hurry. They'll be back in a minute and I want to get the children inside where they'll be safer."

"Who'll be back? Veronica, how did you get so dirty? What's going on?"

"The Japanese will be back. We were at Schofield when the first bombs came, and we tried to get to the hospital, but they've bombed the harbor and now they're coming back. Help me, we've got to hurry."

"Veronica Stewart, I have absolutely no idea what you're talking about."

"The Japanese bombed Pearl Harbor. And they bombed Schofield Barracks. Now they're coming back."

Mrs. Bennett stared at her for a moment, then blinked slowly. She said, "I heard something. It woke me up but I thought it was an explosion or something.

"Pearl Harbor is burning," Veronica said. "And I need your help. They're coming back."

"I'll be just a minute. I have to get dressed."

"Mrs. Bennett, please! They'll be here any minute. Help me! Please!"

Chapter Ten

THEY carried the children to Mrs. Bennett's bedroom and a quick inspection told Veronica what Toshi had already said — only the boy was seriously wounded. Mrs. Bennett called her husband, who brought hot water and clean cloths. Toshi cleaned the wounds of the two children who had been in the back-seat.

Then Mrs. Rhoades looked at Toshi and started screaming, "Get her out of here."

Toshi dropped the cloth as though she'd been shot, and fled from the room.

Mrs. Rhoades then turned on Veronica and screamed, "You get out, too! Why wouldn't you drive us to the hospital?"

"Let me look at your son," Veronica said in as calm a voice as she could manage. "I've had first aid."

"So have I," the woman screamed. "Just get out!"

Mrs. Bennett put her arm around Veronica's shoulder and soothed her as she walked her out of the room. "Just let us handle her, dear. She's obviously distraught and we're old friends, you know."

"Make sure she bandages his head tightly. The wound will probably close of its own accord," Veronica said.

"I can do it without your help," Mrs. Rhoades snapped, though Veronica had been talking to Mrs. Bennett.

Veronica opened her mouth to reply in anger, then she shook her head in dismay. How could she think of quarreling with a woman when they might all be killed in the next few minutes? She could hear bombs dropping in the distance. Poor woman. Her children were wounded, and right now her husband was probably either preparing for battle or he might already be dead. She was ashamed of herself.

Veronica walked from her bedroom out to the lanai where Toshi stood looking at Pearl Harbor below. It was a totally different scene than the one Veronica had shared with Phillip three weeks ago. Smoke rose from fires that burned aboard ships. She wasn't sure how many ships had been hit and she couldn't see the *Arizona* at all. She could only hope it had put out to open sea.

The scene below was confused but she made out things fairly clearly. Only a few of the Japanese planes were in close enough yet to drop bombs. She heard sounds that she assumed were small explosions, and other sounds that sounded like gunshots, though the planes were too far away to be hit. She wondered if the sailors were firing into the empty air.

It was hard to know what the Japanese planes intended to hit this time. So much damage was already done. One large battleship was a blazing inferno. It seemed to be sinking in pieces and she guessed that it had blown apart in the water. Smoke and fire obscured some of her view, but she could see clearly that one battleship would never recover from the earlier blows. Could it be the *Arizona*?

Veronica caught her breath at the thought and then shook her head. She was not going to frighten herself to death with imaginary fears. There were too many real ones. She told herself that the *Arizona* was probably far out at sea by now. But she couldn't help asking herself whether Phillip was down there on one of those burning ships fighting fires. Or was he even still alive? She bit her lip to keep from crying. There was worse to come, and she couldn't break down now.

The sky was swarming with angry Japanese bombers who were getting so close she could hear the sound of their engines. They came from the south and east and they seemed to be heading toward Battleship Row. There should have been seven large battleships sitting on the east side of Ford Island, though she could only see five. They were the heart of the Pacific Fleet and Veronica knew that any of those ships would be a blow to all of the defense of the Pacific.

She knew that the Japanese planes might skip over the harbor and bomb the city this time. By the looks of the damage done below, the Pacific Fleet was already crippled, so they might decide to maim the town as well. Veronica wondered if she would be brave in the face of death. She shut her eyes against the tears and knew that she didn't want to die yet. She was too young — there was too much to live for.

The tears rolled down her cheeks as she realized that she was only a few years younger than most of the young men down there on those ships. Many were dead already and others would die soon. This attack meant war, and war meant death. Waves of nausea washed through her and she thought she might faint at the realization that she was watching the destruction of hundreds, perhaps thousands, of people.

The planes were clearly heading for Pearl Harbor again. The battleships were still the chosen target. Veronica shuddered, wondering how many of them would survive. There were too many planes for Veronica to count, but there were clearly over a hundred. They covered the sky, blotting out the sun.

She looked at her watch. It was eight-forty. Unbelievable as it seemed, all the terrible events that she had witnessed had happened in less than an hour. She'd driven all the way from Schofield just to see more terror played out here in the second attack on Honolulu.

Only one of the battleships below seemed to be moving at all. That one moved slowly past the battleship that was blazing brightest, and next to another battleship that was on fire but not totally out of control. As it continued its journey past the sister ships, another wave of Japanese bombers came in for the kill. Veronica watched in horror as, one by one, the bombers dropped their bombs on the moving target. She counted six bombs, and then the bridge and forestructure of the ship burst into flames.

Now every battleship that she could see was burning and immobilized. They looked exactly like the barracks as Schofield, Veronica thought.

Mrs. Bennett came out and stood beside her on the lanai, watching the destruction below. She asked, "Where are our planes?"

"We don't have any," Veronica answered.

"I don't understand," Mrs. Bennett said. "Pearl Harbor is the best defended harbor in the world."

Another ship explosion rocked the harbor and the sky lit up with a blaze of fire. Veronica could see dark objects being thrown off the ship and wondered what they could be. Then she realized that men were jumping into the water to escape being burned alive.

As they jumped, the sounds of a few guns peppered the sky with ineffectual attempts to fight back, but the bombs kept coming.

Mr. Bennett joined them and watched in silence for a moment, and then he asked, "Where are our planes?"

"We don't have any," Mrs. Bennett answered with a catch in her throat.

"They haven't been able to get off the ground yet," Veronica said. It seemed important not to give up hoping.

"Do you think I should hide my silverware?" Mrs. Bennett asked.

Both girls turned in confusion to the older woman. She explained, "For when the Japanese invade, I mean. Do you think I should hide the valuables? The Nazis are stealing everything from the Europeans."

"Do you think they'll invade?" Toshi asked.

"Of course," Mrs. Bennett answered. "Why else do you think they're bombing this way? They'll take over Hawaii first and use it to attack the States."

Fear gripped Veronica's body. She willed herself not to tremble and to keep her voice calm as she shook her head and said, "They won't try to land in Hawaii. We'd never let them do that."

"We let them do *that*," Mrs. Bennett said, and waved her hand toward Pearl Harbor.

"That was a surprise attack," Toshi said. "We know we're at war now. We'll be prepared for any land invasion."

"There may already be people on this island who are fighting *for* the Japanese. There may be many people who will want the Japanese to win the war." Mrs. Bennett looked uneasily at Toshi.

Toshi's face was grave and determined as she said, "No. The people of Hawaii will fight for every inch of this island. No one will help the Japanese army if they come."

"But there may be spies," Mrs. Bennett said. "If there weren't spies, how could they surprise us this way?"

"I think the city is safe," Veronica said. "We should go on down to the hospital now." She wanted to put her arm around her friend Toshi and protect her from the Bennetts' suspicions. Would everyone in Hawaii react the way Mrs. Bennett and Mrs. Rhoades had? Would they all blame the terrible attack on every person of Japanese ancestry? If so, Hawaii was going to be a very confused place to live.

"We will fight," Toshi answered Mrs. Bennett's accusations fiercely. "My family will fight. My brothers and sisters will fight. We will fight with guns or knives or with our hands. We will not surrender and we will not be shamed."

"I didn't mean you, my dear," Mrs. Bennett said quickly. "I know you're a loyal American, dear. I just meant. . . ." Her sentence trailed off, and she said, "The bombs have stopped. I think they're going."

It was true. The Japanese planes were nearly all gone now, and those few who still circled the harbor were no longer dropping bombs. They seemed merely to be circling to survey the damage below. It was very difficult for Veronica to see because so much heavy black smoke clouded the view. But she could still see flames and she knew that under that black screen, a dreadful scene of destruction still burned.

"They'll be bringing in the wounded. I'd better get to the hospital," Veronica said.

"How do you know they won't be back?" Mrs. Bennett asked.

"Even if they do, it will take them a while to load up their bombs again," Veronica answered.

"But if they land you'll be safer up here in the hills," Mrs. Bennett said.

"We have an ambulance," Veronica answered. "The Red Cross will need it."

"I can't let you go to the hospital," Mrs. Bennett objected. "Your mother would never forgive me for not sending you home."

"My mother is already at the hospital," Veronica said. "That's her emergency station."

"You mean just because she's in the Red Cross she went off and left you?" Mrs. Bennett asked in a shocked voice.

"We're military people," Veronica said proudly. "We do our duty."

"You're just a girl," Mrs. Bennett protested. "At least stay here until the radio comes back on and they tell us what to do."

"I know what to do," Veronica answered. "My emergency station is the hospital, and this is an emergency."

Chapter
Eleven

IT was a short drive from Mrs. Bennett's house to the hospital, but the streets were so crowded and there was so much confusion that it took almost fifteen minutes. During that time, Mrs. Rhoades complained bitterly about the fact that they hadn't driven straight into the city as she'd wanted.

"I'm going to tell your mother," she threatened. Then she added, "My little boy might have died because of your disobedience. You act like you think you're an adult, but you're only a child."

"I'm sixteen," Veronica said. "And I drove us to the hospital as quickly as I thought was safe. Besides, your children aren't seriously hurt." She bit her lip to keep from adding that Mrs. Rhoades had taken an ambulance that might have been better used by more severely wounded people. It would be foolish to continue a quarrel with an overwrought woman. Besides, the ambulance would be put to good use helping the wounded at Pearl Harbor.

They were in the center of the city now, and large groups of people stood around on street corners looking bewildered. There were police directing traffic, and several times Veronica had to pull over to the side so that Army trucks could get by. She was relieved that the Army trucks were moving at all. That meant that not all the American defenses were crippled by the attack.

Now that the Japanese planes were gone, the sky was almost empty. Once or twice Veronica saw an American plane heading out to sea, but it was clear that there was not going to be a massive Air Force retaliation.

Veronica tried hard not to panic about the current military situation. However, she knew enough about military tactics to be really worried. If the Pacific Fleet was destroyed and there were no airplanes in the sky, that meant that there were neither water nor air defenses against an invasion. If the Japanese landed in Hawaii, only the Army would be there to fight them. She wondered how much of the Army was left, and whether they were prepared to fight.

As Mrs. Rhoades carped and complained, Mrs. Bennett's fearful statements rang in her ears. Would the Japanese attempt to land in Hawaii? Would their planes return for another bombing raid?

It was a relief to see the hospital ahead. Veronica slowed as she entered the gates and asked, "Where can I turn in the ambulance?"

"You carrying wounded?"

"From Schofield Barracks," Veronica said, "but they can walk."

"Schofield! They got Schofield, too?"

"Yes."

"They hit them all, then."

"What about the other islands? Maui?" she asked.

But he didn't know anything. "They turned the radio off about two hours ago. Nothing but the police station now." He directed Veronica to the main entrance where she let off Mrs. Rhoades and her children. The woman gathered her three children together and rushed through the doors of the hospital without saying either good-bye or thank you.

Veronica turned to Toshi and asked, "Can you walk home from here? I should turn the ambulance in."

"I'll call home," Toshi said. "But I'm going to work at the hospital with you."

"You're not in the Red Cross," Veronica said. Then she smiled in bitter memory. Had it only been a month since she herself had said the Red Cross was a lot of foolish nonsense, and had begged to be let off from attending the meetings?

"I want to help," Toshi said. "If they'll let me."

"They'll let you," Veronica promised her, but she dreaded the moment when Toshi reported for duty. Both Mrs. Bennett and Mrs. Rhoades had said terrible things about the Japanese, or "Japs," as they called them. Maybe other adults at the hospital would feel that way. It wasn't fair but then war wasn't fair. The Japanese surprise attack had taught them that this morning.

It seemed as though there were so many awful things going on all at once that it was difficult to think about any one thing for very long. She told herself that she'd already forgotten Mrs. Rhoades and her ungrateful rudeness. In a few minutes she would probably be wondering why she'd been worried about whether or not they'd give Toshi a job. She nodded to her friend and said, "Okay. Let's go."

She parked the ambulance at the side door of the hospital and got out, looking around for someone who was in charge. A young man ran up to her and called out, "You have wounded in back?"

"No."

He ran on to another ambulance that was pulling in. As it had been just about everywhere else she'd been that morning, there were a lot of people milling around in confusion with dazed looks on their faces. But most of the people here seemed to have a definite purpose. People in hospital or military uniforms were running back and forth, calling out orders to each other.

She watched as the young man who spoke to her directed two other young men who lifted a stretcher out of the back of an ambulance. They seemed to know what they were doing. It made her feel hopeful to know that not everyone was totally unprepared.

She could hear sirens calling from many different directions. They sounded as though they were coming from all over the city and there was the smell of smoke in the air. She saw a police captain standing on the sidewalk and she walked over to him, asking, "This is an ambulance from Schofield. Where can I put it?"

"You drive it?"

"Yes."

"Take it to the harbor. They'll tell you what to do."

"I'm not an ambulance driver," Veronica protested.

"Didn't you drive in from Schofield?"

"Yes."

"Then you're an ambulance driver. Get going."

Veronica turned to Toshi and asked, "Come with me?"

"Go alone," the policeman ordered. "She'll only take up space." Then added, "You'd better get inside, girlie, or go home."

"Is there trouble?" Veronica asked. She realized that asking whether or not there was trouble might seem foolish on this day, but the policeman seemed to understand her question. It was entirely possible that people would try to take revenge on their own Japanese people because they couldn't catch the Japanese bombers.

"No trouble yet," the policeman warned. "But people are talking crazy today. Better for Japs to stay off the street." Veronica and Toshi both winced at his use of the word "Japs," but they didn't argue with him He was right, people were crazy today.

Toshi said, "I'll go inside. I'll tell your mother you're all right. She'll give me a job."

Veronica nodded and went back to the ambulance. The ambulance seemed larger than she remembered it and she knew it was because she was in it all alone. At times, as she drove through the streets, she felt like she was inside one of the battleships she'd seen sunk in the harbor. She inched her way through the congested traffic toward the waterfront. More than once she passed by barricades that were put up to keep the roads clear for emergency traffic. She only had to stop once as a series of six ambulances raced by with their sirens going full blast. She knew they were racing toward the hospital and she couldn't help wondering if Phillip was in one of those screaming cars.

It seemed to take an incredible amount of time, but when she got to the waterfront, she looked at her watch and it was only ten in the morning. Veronica sighed as she realized that the whole nightmare had only been two hours long. She moved slowly through the confusion on the street, threading her way through the ambulances and army trucks that made up most of the traffic. Twice she passed men in swimsuits who were walking toward the docks, and she wondered if they could actually be crazy enough to be going swimming today. But then nearly everything seemed crazy today.

At dockside she found a place to park behind two other ambulances, and jumped out of the ambulance. She ran up to the driver in front, asking, "Do you know what I should do with this ambulance?"

"Wait here. They're bringing them out of the water as fast as they can." He pointed to the water's edge where soldiers, sailors, and men in swimsuits were all working together to pull someone over the edge of the dock.

It was difficult to see much because of the smoke that hung over the docks like a heavy cloud of hopelessness. She knew the water was out there beyond the blackness, and once in a while she glimpsed flames when the smoke thinned. The ships were still burning and the men in swimsuits were attempting to rescue sailors who went overboard into the dark waters. She knew that most Mainlanders didn't swim very well and that many would escape the bombs and flames only to drown. She guessed that most of the rescue workers were Hawaiians, whose phenomenal swimming abilities were known all over the world.

She thought of Phillip again and fear enveloped her. Where was he? Was he alive?

The smoke from the fires got thicker and she began to have trouble breathing. The sailors who were loading her ambulance with men on stretchers were covered with black soot. They looked exhausted. As they lifted the first man, one of the sailors said, "Drive fast."

She looked down at the three men on stretchers and her heart did a flip-flop. One looked absolutely white, and she was sure he was dead. The other was so badly burned that she doubted that he would live. Only one was conscious and he stared at her with wide blue eyes as he moaned softly under his breath. "Are you going with me?" Veronica asked one of the sailors.

"No. And get back as fast as you can because the Hawaiians are reporting in fast."

Another sailor shook his head and said, "Those guys swim like sharks. They're bringing our men in two at a time."

"And they're not afraid of fire," his buddy added. "They're swimming through burning oil to get the wounded out. We'll have a lot more out of the water when you get back."

She tried not to wince as they lifted the palest man into the ambulance. Was there a chance that he was alive? He looked dead but she wasn't sure. "How many were killed?" Veronica asked.

The second sailor shrugged and said, "Hundreds, so far."

"Hundreds," Veronica repeated.

"Thousands," the other sailor corrected. Then he clapped Veronica on the shoulder and said, "Get going, Red."

She drove with her siren on and made the trip as fast as she could, but when she got there she was pretty sure that at least one of her passengers was dead. She stood quietly beside the ambulance as they unloaded the wounded sailors. Only the one with the light blue eyes was still conscious and he looked at her with pure fear shining from his pale eyes. She turned away from his gaze and asked the sailors, "Do I go back again?"

"I guess so," one answered. "You're an ambulance driver, aren't you?"

"Sort of," Veronica admitted and turned back to the ambulance again. It was better not to worry about how many of the victims were alive or dead. Her job was to bring them to the hospital — that was all.

She made three trips during the next hour and then she looked at the gas gauge. The needle hovered just above empty. At the hospital she asked where she could get gas, and the same policeman told her she'd better go to the shipyards and ask Captain Smollett, who was in charge of the ambulances. She wondered how Captain Smollett got that job. He worked with her father and as far as she knew, he'd never done anything but desk work. He was one of those naval officers who thought he wasn't doing anything important unless he was actually on a ship, and he complained long and loud about the "landlubber" jobs he'd had in Hawaii.

Captain Smollett recognized her in spite of the fact that she was covered with black soot, and she felt a thousand years older than she'd been the last time they met. "Veronica, where's your father?"

"Dad's on Maui," she said. "He's not due back till tomorrow."

"Why aren't you home with your mother?"

"Mother's in the hospital at her Red Cross station," she replied. "I'm driving an ambulance."

"We can't have that. Where did you learn to drive an ambulance?"

"I learned this morning," Veronica answered. "I was at Schofield when it was bombed, and the ambulance was stalled. So I started it and then drove it. But I need gas now."

"How old are you?" he asked. Captain Smollett looked distracted and white-faced. His fingers flipped through papers as he talked to her, but his eyes were on something much farther away.

"Sixteen."

"You're too young," he said. "Turn the ambulance in and go home. Your father would never forgive me if you were killed."

"I won't be killed," Veronica said. "The bombing is over."

"For now," Captain Smollett said. "We expect them back any minute, Veronica. Believe me, they'll be back and this time it won't be a sneak attack. We'll be ready for them."

"Maybe they won't come back," Veronica said. "Didn't they already hit all the targets they were after?"

"This is war, and when they get here, I want you under cover. Turn the ambulance in."

"Let me fill it with gas first," she said. "I hate to waste time for some other driver. Besides, I'm not sure I have enough gas to get back to the hospital."

"There's a storage tank and a pump at Dock B. Can you find that?"

"Yes."

"I was playing golf this morning when the bombs hit," Captain Smollett said suddenly, as Veronica started to leave. "We saw them coming but it was too late to warn anyone. Two hours ago I was teeing off, now I'm directing ambulances that are bringing in burned bodies."

Veronica was startled to see tears begin to run down his cheeks. She said, "I'm sorry, sir."

"Get going, girl. Get your gas and get back to safety. That's an order."

"As long as I'm here, I might as well pick up some more wounded," Veronica said.

"You're a brave girl, Veronica."

She waited for a moment for him to actually give permission, but he stared over her head out the tiny glass window at the water beyond. Veronica knew he was watching the Pacific Fleet burn and that he was grieving.

It took almost thirty minutes to get gas from the Navy supply because there were several other vehicles in front of her and the young sailor who was operating the pumps seemed so inept. He had obviously never pumped gas before and he dropped the hose twice while Veronica watched him. She was so numb and tired that she barely noticed the fact that gasoline was running all over the floor of the station. What would have signaled danger earlier was just a part of life now.

When it was Veronica's turn to get gas, the sailor said, "I can only give you five gallons."

"But this is an ambulance," she protested.

"Can't help it. Them's my orders."

"Fill up the tank," Veronica ordered. "It's foolish not to."

"There's too many ambulances. They all need gas," he protested.

"Why take an ambulance out of service for thirty minutes and then only give five gallons of gas? Three trips and I'll be back in line."

"Those are my orders."

"I'll tell my father," Veronica threatened. "His name is Captain Charles Stewart, and he'll be very angry."

"Is your father really a Navy captain?" the young sailor asked.

"Yes, and I'm sure you don't want me to report you," Veronica answered. "Now fill it up."

As he pumped the gas, she asked, "Where were you when the Japanese bombed?"

"Right here," he said. "And boy, was I scared. I'm still scared. Do you think they'll come back?"

"I don't know."

"I heard they landed at Ewa Beach already. How far is that?"

"Close," Veronica said. "I don't think they landed there. What does the radio say?"

"Nothing. It's off the air. Once in a while someone comes on and asks for blood donors or something, but there's no real news."

He put the cap back on the gas tank, and she said, "Good luck."

"You, too," he said. Then they both stared at each other for a moment as though wishing each other luck had made them good friends. He reached out and touched her hair and said, "Pretty," then he let his hand drop and she drove away.

As she drove, she thought of Phillip. He had called her hair rose gold. Where was he now? Was he alive or dead? Would she ever see him again?

She pulled into her place at the dock and got out of the ambulance to tell the soldiers that she was ready to take another load of wounded to the hospital. As she approached the emergency first aid station a voice called out to her, "Ronnie, over here."

She turned and ran toward him, calling, "Mike! Mike, where are you?"

He was standing on the edge of the dock, holding a quart of milk in one hand and a donut in the other. As she drew close, he put his arms around her and held her close for a second. She felt the comfort and warmth of his body despite the fact that he was very wet. They held each other silently for a minute, then he backed off and said, "Got you all wet. I'm sorry."

"What are you doing?" she asked, then she answered her own question. "You're bringing in the sailors. How long have you been here?"

"About three hours," Mike said. "I was listening to the radio and I heard the bombs. At first we thought it was another drill but the radio announcer kept saying, 'This is the real McCoy,' so I came on down. When I got here, there were already a bunch of other Hawaiians."

"Did you start swimming while they were still bombing?"

"Sure. We all did."

Veronica shook her head and said, "I thought *I* was brave. I wouldn't swim into a bombing attack."

"Hawaiians will swim anywhere," Mike said, and then he laughed because that was the kind of thing that tourists would say.

It was a short laugh and his face sobered quickly as he asked, "What are you doing?"

"I've been driving an ambulance," Veronica said. "Oh, Mike, it's awful. They all look like they're just about our age, and I think a lot of the ones I've brought to the hospital are already dead."

"I know," Mike said. "I've fished a lot of guys out and about half of them are already gone."

"How bad do you think it is, Mike? Are any of our battleships left?"

"Most are hit but we may save some." Then he asked quietly, "You know the *Arizona* went down, Ronnie, don't you?"

"She sank?" Veronica steadied her balance by leaning on Mike's arm. He was still wet from the sea and she could feel that he was getting cold. But he seemed like the only solid thing left in her world. She was very glad he was here with her.

"She's sinking," Mike said. "Burning and sinking at the same time. We can't get close to her, Ronnie."

"Is everyone . . ."

"Can't tell for sure but it looks like a total loss." Mike's hands were strong as he held her upright. "We're pulling in a few of them but they're all burned to a crisp."

Veronica shook her head, "They can't all be dead. Some will survive."

"Maybe," Mike said quietly. "But I thought you ought to know."

"I don't know," Veronica said, tilting her

chin high. "All I know is that some of the men are dead. I don't know that Phillip is even hurt. I'm not going to believe that until I absolutely have to, Mike."

"All right, Ronnie. I'm sorry."

"You don't need to be sorry," Veronica said. "You didn't bomb anyone. You're doing your best to save people. Maybe you'll save Phillip, Mike. You're a good, strong swimmer, you might be able to. Mike, promise me you'll try."

"I'll try, Ronnie." He bent and kissed her swiftly on the cheek and then he dove back into the water. The black water and smoke swallowed him quickly. Veronica turned and went back to her ambulance. There was work to do.

Chapter Twelve

SHE didn't give up the ambulance until she saw that there was really another driver for it. When the tall, thin Texas boy in an Army uniform took the keys from her, he sensed her reluctance to release the machine. "You don't need to worry about this ambulance, ma'am. I'll take care of it for you."

Veronica nodded and handed him the keys. "There are so many wounded." Her voice cracked and she shuddered. "A lot of them are burned. From the floating oil, you know. The oil rides on the surface of the water and it catches fire. They burn or they drown. . . ."

The Texas boy put his arm around her and said, "You can just rest now, little lady. I'll take over. You're just a pretty little girl. It's natural that you're all tuckered out."

His patronizing attitude made her furious. He was talking to her as though she was a child. Didn't he know she'd been doing a man's job? Veronica drew away from him, and said, "I am not tired. I was just upset thinking about the wounded. I'll be all right, and thank you for taking over."

As she walked away, she realized that it was easier to keep moving if she was mad. The anger blotted out the fear and discouragement. Was that why Mrs. Rhoades had been so miserable this morning? Had she hidden her fear with anger?

Once inside the hospital, she dropped all thought of ambulance drivers or passengers. The scene that she walked into was all-consuming and she realized that she must find some way to help the hundreds of wounded who crowded the halls of the hospital. They sat on benches, filled waiting rooms, and lay on stretchers along the edges of the corridors. Some sat on the floor trying to hush crying children. Others stared vacantly ahead, looking at nothing.

One walk through the hospital corridors erased any doubt about the range of the Japanese attack. There were wounded sailors and soldiers, but there were also many civilians who were hurt or dying.

Unlike the scene on the docks, the hospital seemed very organized. Nurses in white uniforms looked crisp and efficient as they strode down the halls. There were other women who followed in street clothes. Some wore Red Cross armbands. Veronica recognized several members of her Red Cross chapter.

She stopped three Red Cross workers before she learned that her mother was setting up an emergency blood bank at the other end of the hospital. It was Shirley Wilson, a young lieutenant's wife, who told her, "So many of the men need blood transfusions, and we're running out of plasma. They broadcast an appeal for blood about ten minutes ago, and your mother is in charge of setting up the blood bank."

Veronica found the blood bank very easily because as she walked through the wings of the hospital, she heard several people ask, "Where's the blood bank?"

By the time she found her mother, she was in the company of about fifteen other people, all of whom were ready to donate. Her mother hugged her fiercely for about thirty seconds and asked. "You're not hurt?"

"No. Tired, but not hurt."

"You'll be more tired in a few hours," Annabelle Stewart said. "I'm glad you're here because now I know I have at least one person I can count on."

It pleased her to be praised by her mother, but she merely nodded and asked, "Did Toshi get here?"

"Toshi's been helping for two hours. We worked in the emergency room for a while and then they asked me to set up the donor bank, and I asked Toshi to be in charge of the cafeteria."

"Cafeteria?"

"We turned the cafeteria in this wing into

an emergency laboratory. She's washing plasma bottles and tubing," Annabelle explained. "It's a job that takes meticulous attention and it keeps her away from people."

A man and woman in bright yellow-print shirts and white slacks came up to them, and the woman said, "Is this where they take the blood?"

"Yes," Annabelle answered. "Just get in line over there. We'll be ready soon."

"I'm ready now," the woman said. "I want to give as much as you'll take. So hurry up, there's a long line."

Annabelle and Veronica turned to look where the man was pointing and Annabelle smiled, "The radio appeal must have worked. Look at that."

There were at least fifty men and women standing in line now, and other groups of people were walking down the hall. Annabelle said, "Veronica, you might as well screen the line. Just walk down the line and sort out the ones over sixty or under sixteen. Ask the others about their health and send anyone with any chronic diseases home."

"Don't I need an armband or uniform or something?"

"I'll see what I can find," Annabelle said. "Now be sure and be pleasant to everyone. Remember you're Captain Charles Stewart's daughter."

"Yes, mother." For once, Veronica didn't argue with her mother, nor was she angry at the admonition. Her mother hugged her quickly and started away. Veronica stopped her with a question. "Mother?"

"What?"

"Do you think the Japanese will come back?"

"Yes." Her mother looked at her with honest, level eyes and a calm gaze. "I believe they will press their advantage, either with more bombing raids or an attempted landing."

"Do you think the Japanese can win?"

"Not in the long run," her mother answered. "You've heard your father talk often enough about the fact that they've neither the men, materials, nor resources to win in China. They probably attacked us because they felt their battle in the Far East was hopeless unless they got more raw materials. They were losing in China and they'll be hopelessly mismatched against the United States." She paused and then said softly, "I do believe it's possible they may take the Hawaiian Islands, Veronica. I won't lie to you about that."

"What can we do?" Veronica asked.

"Exactly what we are doing," her mother answered. "Our duty. I'm very proud of you, dear, and I love you. Remember that."

They hugged again and went to their separate jobs. As Veronica walked down the hall, she realized that it had been a long time since her mother had said she loved her. Even in the midst of all this terror and turmoil there was something to feel good about. But even though she felt closer to her mother than she had since she was a small child, she missed her father desperately and wanted him to get home from Maui as quickly as possible.

Interviewing people to see if they were going to be accepted as blood donors wasn't difficult, but it was a tiresome job. People asked her so many questions she couldn't answer. Many of them asked about the impending invasion by Japanese troops. Most wanted official clarification of the rumors they'd been hearing.

"Did you hear the Japs landed at San Francisco?" one woman asked.

"I heard it was Los Angeles," her friend corrected.

"And the Germans are in New York," another one of the trio insisted.

"Don't you think we should wait for official word before we worry about that? None of the radio stations are on the air," Veronica said. The rumors they were repeating seemed preposterous, but a few hours ago she would have said it was preposterous that the Japanese could bomb Pearl Harbor with absolutely no resistance.

"I heard it from my neighbor," the first woman admitted. "Course, you can't trust anything she says. What are they telling you here in the hospital?"

"Nothing," Veronica said crisply. "We just do our job and try not to worry about things we can't control."

As she walked up and down the line, giving instructions and asking questions, she was very aware that in other parts of the hospital there were people doing even more important emergency work. The rumors of impending invasion mixed with personal accounts of tragedy to form a picture of an island-wide disaster.

As more people came in off the streets to donate blood, they brought new rumors and facts with them. The horror stories piled up, one on top of the other, until Veronica thought she could hear no more.

She thought about Phillip as little as possible because each time she began to worry about him, the certainty that he was dead became stronger. The dread she felt about hearing for certain gradually softened, and she began to listen for news of the *Arizona* and its crew. Everything she heard confirmed what Mike had told her earlier in the day.

"It cracked right in half and sank," one man told her.

"Weighs thirty-two thousand tons, and it split open like a melon," his friend added. "They all died, they say. Every one of them."

Later, she began to worry about Mike as well, because she heard that several of the Hawaiian swimmers were badly burned. "Those fools just swam right through the burning oil, and when they got the sailors out, they were all dead. Second degree burns, I hear. About six out of commission."

It was easy to imagine that Mike was one

of the burned swimmers. He would be brave enough to do a thing like that. She tried to turn her mind back to her work, but dread of hearing about either of her boyfriends gnawed at the fabric of the tight cover she kept on her emotions.

And then she heard something that made her afraid for her father. A woman in the line told her she'd decided to donate blood while she waited for her sister to receive emergency treatment for a cut knee. "It's not too bad, but the nurse said she should have it stitched up. We were on a fishing boat off the island of Maui and a Japanese plane fired on the boat. I think it landed there."

Until this moment, she'd assumed that her father was probably safe on Maui, but now she began to worry about him. She knew there were millions of rumors going around, but what if the Japanese really had landed there? What if he'd been wounded or killed in the fighting? What if . . . ? Veronica shook her head and said out loud, "I just think the best thing we can do is not worry about things we aren't sure about. We have enough to do right here, don't we?"

She tried to maintain a detached distance from all the rumors she heard on the blood donor line. It got harder to do as she became physically tired. And the rumors did get stranger as time went on. She heard everything. Someone told her the Japanese Embassy was full of a small army that planned to take over in the middle of the night. Someone else swore that the Japanese hadn't really attacked at all, that it was the Germans in disguise.

From time to time, Veronica glanced at her watch, and she was surprised at how quickly the time seemed to be going. Earlier in the morning, during the bombing raids, so much happened so fast that ten minutes seemed like an hour. Then when she'd been driving the ambulance she'd raced against time to get the wounded into the hospital. Now the blood donor work kept her busy, but there wasn't the sense of immediate emergency. Instead of slowing down, time seemed to speed by. Before she knew it, her watch said it was five o'clock in the afternoon.

A nurse came by about six and told her to go downstairs to get something to eat.

"I'm not hungry."

"But you'll need your strength for the night," the nurse pointed out. "That is, if you can work a little longer."

"I can work," she answered. She dreaded stopping even for a minute because she knew if she stopped she would begin to worry about the possibility of the Japanese invading, about Phillip, about Mike, and about her father. Work was the only alternative to worry.

Chapter Thirteen

INSTEAD of going to the large cafeteria where the Red Cross women were feeding hospital workers, Veronica went to the small cafeteria which had become an emergency laboratory for the blood bank. There were several women in white coats who were very intent on their job of cleaning the glass bottles and tubes used for blood transfusions. She found Toshi bending over a huge sink, rinsing glass tubing in boiling hot water. She finished rinsing one tube and held it up to the light to see if it was absolutely clean. Toshi had a burn on her arm, and two Band-Aids covered where she'd been cut by broken glass. Her black hair was pulled back off her face by a white scarf, and she looked pale and tired. She was so intent on her work that she didn't see Veronica come in and sink into an empty chair behind her.

When she did turn around, Veronica asked, "Want to go for supper?"

Toshi shook her head. "Someone brought me a sandwich."

"Come have a Coke. You look like you need a rest."

"My back hurts, that's all." Toshi put her hands on her hips and bent backwards to relieve the muscle tension caused from bending over the sink for hours.

"You're lucky you're short," one of the other workers said. "It's worse if you're tall."

"Yes," Toshi agreed quickly and then asked Veronica, "How's your mother doing?"

"She's fine. Working hard, but fine. Did you see your folks?"

Toshi frowned quickly and said, "They can't find out anything about my uncle's family. We heard that several civilians were killed near Schofield."

"You know there are a lot of rumors running around," Veronica cautioned. Her heart sank at the thought of Helen and her family in danger. There were just too many people she knew who were on the potential casualty list.

"My brother came by two hours ago. He was riding his bicycle over there this afternoon. He should be back soon. No cars can get through because the roads are jammed. We were lucky this morning."

"It's because so few people knew the Japs attacked," Veronica said. Then she saw the pain on Toshi's face and she corrected herself. "Japanese, I'm sorry. I've just been listening to people — "

"I know," Toshi said shortly and turned back to her bottle-washing.

"Toshi, don't be mad at me. We've got to stick together. Things are so hard without friends."

Toshi turned back and smiled. "I'm not mad. I just want to get my work done. It's not much but I think if everyone does what he or she can, we can win this war. Don't you?"

"Of course. I saw Mike at the docks. He's swimming out to the sinking ships to pick up wounded sailors. A lot of people are volunteering to do what they can. We'll win this war fast, you'll see. And don't worry, your family will be all right."

Suddenly, the little radio that sat on the edge of the metal table blared out an announcement. "Please turn out your lights. Please turn out all lights. Hawaii is observing a complete blackout. This means the whole territory. Turn out your lights, and do not turn them on for any purpose whatsoever. Turn off your lights and keep them off."

Almost immediately, two men came in with heavy black paper and began sealing the windows. Veronica said, "You'd better go home now because you won't be able to find your way in the dark."

"I can walk in the dark," Toshi said. "But I'm worried about my brother. He can't ride a bicycle at night with no lights to guide him."

"There's nothing to do but wait for news. I guess waiting is the hardest part of war," Veronica said.

"Yes. Everytime the radio comes on, my heart falls to my feet," Toshi admitted. "When General Short came on at 4:30 and said he was putting the islands under martial law, I was so relieved I almost cried. I thought he was going to say we'd been invaded."

"No solid news of any land invasion or any more bombings. I think we saw the real enemy action this morning," Veronica said.

"The nurses and helpers who come in here say everyone in the hospital thinks we'll have another bombing raid tonight. They're prepared for the worst. What do you hear at the blood bank?"

"I try not to listen. I can think up enough things to worry about without listening to rumors." Tears rushed to her eyes, and she allowed herself to feel some of the grief she'd been repressing all day. "Do those nurses have any news at all about the *Arizona*?"

"Just that it went down first," Toshi said. "I don't think they've found any survivors at all."

"Phillip was so sure he'd stay in Hawaii forever," Veronica said bitterly. "Only he thought he'd be going to college and marrying me, not sinking with the Pacific Fleet. You never met him, did you?"

"No. But maybe I will," Toshi said. "Don't give up hope yet, Veronica. It doesn't help."

"What *does* help?"

"To stay strong and work hard. To do everything you can to help the war effort. Never to give up believing that the best can happen. All those things help."

"You're right," Veronica got up from the chair where she'd been sitting, and said, "So I guess I'll go get something to eat and then get back to work. It may be a long night."

It was seven P.M. when she left the cafeteria and went back to her post at the blood bank. As she walked down the long corridors, she decided that the last twelve hours had been longer than her first sixteen years. This morning when she woke, she'd been full of plans for college and her biggest problem had been which boy to date. Now there probably wouldn't be a college choice, and one of the boys was almost certainly dead.

When she got back to the blood bank the line was shorter than it had been earlier in the day. She saw several people whom she remembered from the morning, but she let them pass through without argument. No one was supposed to donate blood more than once every twenty-four hours, but these people probably felt it was the only thing they could do to help.

Since many men were engaged in some other sort of emergency activity, most of the people in the line were women. She'd learned earlier in the day that women's blood was richer in plasma and better, anyway.

A group of Hawaiian swimmers came in about seven o'clock and to her great relief Veronica saw that Mike was with them. They came as a group, swaggering a little, and making jokes about the free brandy they'd heard the blood bank gave away to donors. Most of them were in their early twenties and as healthy looking as any people could be, but she saw that a few were older, in their thirties and forties. They must have been exhausted by the long hours of swimming, but they all pretended to be having the time of their lives.

All of them seemed to be perfectly at ease in the hospital in spite of the fact that they wore only swimsuits and had bare feet. They walked and talked like royalty, and everyone turned to smile at them when they came in the door. Their presence seemed to light up the hospital corridor. People listened eagerly to their jokes and seemed to take courage from the fact that they were out in the water, protecting Hawaii.

"Is it true you caught a submarine with your bare hands?" one man asked.

"Not true," the oldest Hawaiian said. "I used a knife."

"And a fork," his companion added. "We don't want to have the Japs think we have bad manners before we eat them up."

Like all the others, Mike had patches of black soot from the fires on his face, but to Veronica, he had never looked more handsome. She saw that he had small burns on both his arms, and her first words to him were, "You should have those burns treated."

"The salt water is good for burns," he said. "Think you can use some Hawaiian blood in your bank?"

"Sure," Veronica answered, and then she smiled. Only last week she and her mother had quarreled when she used that word instead of certainly. She promised herself that she would never quarrel over unimportant things again. "Are you finished at the docks?"

"We had to come out of the water because it was so dark, but we can start swimming again when the moon comes up. How long do we have to wait in line?"

"I'll get you right in." All day long, she'd been putting the men who took time off from their critical jobs on the docks at the head of the line. No one ever complained. "Are you sure you and your friends have the strength to do this?"

"Sure." Mike grinned at her and said, "It's good to see you, Ronnie."

"Mike, was it awful?"

He looked straight into her eyes and said, "Pretty awful. Tomorow morning we start trying to cut the ones who are trapped out of the sinking ships. That will be worse."

"Mike. . . ." Her voice faltered as she asked the dreaded question. "Did you find Phillip?"

"No, Ronnie. I asked for him, but you've got to remember there are thousands of men out there. They say we've got over two thousand dead and another thousand wounded. I personally must have dragged out a hundred men."

"You must be exhausted."

He shook his head and said, "We're just getting started. We can't afford to be exhausted yet."

At that moment, the scene in the hospital corridor changed subtly. Veronica knew something was wrong, though she couldn't have said exactly why. The clues were small: nurses who went by walked at a faster pace, and the Red Cross women began whispering to each other. Others must have sensed it also because all talk died down and people looked up at the ceiling as they listened for sounds that they dreaded hearing.

There was the sound of anti-aircraft guns coming from the direction of Pearl Harbor, and the faint sound of airplanes overhead. Veronica's knees tightened in preparation for the attack that she knew was coming. Her heart began racing and her mind replayed the scenes she'd seen at Schofield and Pearl Harbor this morning.

She turned to Mike and whispered, "They're bombing us again."

He nodded and reached out to take her hand, saying, "I've had first aid. I can help with the wounded."

"Red Cross?" she asked.

"Boy Scouts," he answered, and they

smiled at each other as they held hands and waited for the bombs to drop.

There was the sound of more anti-aircraft guns and then something that sounded like an explosion, followed by another loud sound. At each blast, Veronica felt fear rise in her stomach and clutch her throat. She wanted to turn and run, but there was no place to run to.

Veronica fought hard against the fear that threatened to overwhelm her. She knew that anger could be turned to energy that could be used to fight, but that fear would destroy her. She bit her lip and whispered to herself, "I'll fight to the end. I'll shoot a gun or use a knife, but I'll never give up."

The anti-aircraft guns were silent, and Mike let go of her hand, saying, "Thanks for letting me hold onto you. I'm scared of the dark."

"I don't think you and your friends are scared of anything," Veronica said. She didn't confide that she'd just put up a fierce battle against terror.

"Sure, we're scared," Mike answered. "But we'd fight for this island with our bare hands if we had to. They'll never take Hawaii unless they kill every Hawaiian first."

Gradually, the tension lessened in the hospital corridor and activity returned to normal. Annabelle Stewart found time to come out from behind the donor table and speak to Veronica and Mike. She told them, "We have a radio set up in the back room and someone monitoring it all the time. She came out at seven-fifteen and told us the police radio station said we were being bombed again. But it couldn't have been a full-fledged raid."

Mike and his swimmer friends donated their blood and slipped out into the darkness. Before he left, Mike squeezed her hand and said, "Keep your chin up, Ronnie."

"Be careful, Mike." She hated to let Mike go because the fear was back, whispering to her that this might be the last time she'd ever see him. There had been so many losses this day, it was almost logical to expect another.

Chapter
Fourteen

THERE were no more bombs that night, though they heard gunfire from time to time. There was a total blackout of the city, of course, so it was forbidden to look out the windows to see what was happening or where the gunfire was coming from. Only a few army trucks and ambulances moved in the dark streets. They brought the few wounded sailors who made it to shore alone to the hospital.

Inside the hospital there was plenty of light, and the entrances were rigged up in graduated blackness so that a person who went out the doors had to first pass through a pitch back hallway to get out. About midnight, Veronica walked Toshi down that long black corridor so she could go home. "I know my brother is in trouble," Toshi said. "Or else he would have come to tell me about my

uncle's family. He's still out there somewhere, and my parents must be very worried.
I'm sorry, but I must go."

"You'll sleep better at home," Veronica
said. "And you can come back in the morning if you want."

"I'll be back," Toshi promised.

They held hands until they finished the
long walk and opened the door onto the night.
They were startled because it was much
lighter outside than it had been inside. A
large moon shone over Hawaii, lighting the
landscape almost as well as the city lights
would have.

"Some blackout," Veronica said.

"At least I'll be able to find my way home
safely," Toshi said. Then she pointed to the
rainbow that circled the moon and said,
"Look at that."

The lunar rainbow was spectacular, with
all the daytime colors softened and subdued
by the warm night air. It gave off a glow that
was mostly rose-colored. As they watched the
moon shimmer, Veronica whispered, "That's
a sign of victory. The ancient Hawaiians all
believed that when a rainbow shown over
the moon before battle, it meant they would
win."

"We'll win," Toshi said, and slipped into
the darkness.

Veronica stayed outside for a few minutes, smelling the flowers and breathing the
fresh air. But the floral scents of the warm
night catapulted her back to the evening not

so long ago when her father had called her inside. "The flowers will be there in the morning," he had promised her.

Her breath came in ragged sobs as she remembered her father's laughing words. Would the flowers be there tomorrow? Who could tell? Would any of them be there? What would happen to Toshi and Mike? Was Phillip gone for good? And why wasn't her father back by now?

Suddenly, she was a little girl again, and she wanted her father by her side. She sobbed into the night, calling, "Daddy, Daddy, where are you?"

Then she turned and ran as fast as she could down the dark corridor and into the familar half darkness of the blood bank corridor. She looked frantically for her mother and found her wheeling a portable table over to one side. Annabelle Stewart turned and said, "I thought we could sleep right here on the floor if we just clear out a few things. Will you help me?"

Veronica choked back the tears and helped her mother clear a space on the floor. All around them, hospital workers and volunteer Red Cross women sat against the walls or lay down on the cold corridor floor, trying to get a few hours sleep before the day broke and the second day's work began.

If Annabelle knew that Veronica was crying, she must have decided that it was best to ignore it. They lay down on the floor and her mother asked, "Toshi got off?"

"She's worried about her uncle and Helen. They say some civilians were killed at Schofield. And her brother rode out on his bicycle to find out what happened, and never came back."

"Poor child," Annabelle Stewart murmured. "This is doubly hard on her and her people."

"Because now everyone will hate all Japanese, no matter if they're American-born or not."

"Not all people. Only a few of the ignorant," Annabelle said.

Veronica sighed in relief. If her mother was being this sensible, then others would be. Not everyone was going crazy with hatred that would be taken out on innocent people. But she knew that there was a lot of bad feeling toward the Japanese, because she'd heard the things people were saying. "Maybe I should have walked with her. I hope she gets home all right," Veronica said.

"She's home in bed fast asleep. And you'd better go to sleep yourself," her mother advised. "You'll need your strength for tomorrow."

"I just hope I can sleep," Veronica said. That was the last thing she remembered until dawn, when she was awakened by antiaircraft fire.

She jumped up and ran to the window to see what was happening, but the windows were still covered with black paper. Others had heard the gunfire and most of them rose to stand by the windows. They listened with their heads tilted and their bodies leaning into the sound. Exactly as the night before, there were no bombs, just sporadic gunfire. Finally, the fighting faded and people grabbed donuts and coffee and got to work. By five-thirty, the blood bank was ready to receive the first donors.

The radio was less silent the second morning, but there still wasn't much news. Every few minutes an official would get on the air and call for help. All government workers were ordered to report for active duty even if they were civilians. Men were called in for various jobs — electricians, engineers, stevedores, and mechanics were all asked to report to the shipyards.

Very little actual news came over the radio, but the people who arrived early in the morning to donate blood were full of hearsay. From them, Veronica heard that no bombings had been reported during the night. She also learned that there were several civilians shot by mistake.

One man told her about his neighbor's fatal encounter with the military. "Poor dumb guy was walking home from work, and he was so nervous he forgot and lit a cigarette. Military police saw the light and shot him three times. He's in the hospital now with bullet holes in two legs and an arm."

She learned that the Army had worked all night setting up emergency barricades along the beaches. "They expected a land invasion last night, and they're sure there will be one tonight. Fellow I met says there's already Jap soldiers on Maui," one man told her.

Though she doubted most of the tales, the ones about a landing on Maui kept recurring, and she feared there might be some truth to them. Was her father all right? She knew it was pointless to worry when there was nothing she could do, but she couldn't help coming back to thoughts of her father and Phillip.

Veronica heard other news that was even more worrisome. It was now definite that Pearl Harbor and Schofield weren't the only places that saw action. The Waipahu and Ewa sugar plantations took almost as severe a beating as Pearl Harbor. At Waipahu the fighting started fires in the cane fields, and the guns strafed the terrified workers.

"They came running out of those fields like a flock of birds," a plantation worker told her. "Mostly women and children were hit because that's what was there. And then the bombs hit the plantation hospital and sugar mill. Went right through the roof of the company store. The electric supply warehouse exploded, and there's holes as big as a house all over the pineapple fields. It's a sight out that way."

"Was anyone killed?" Veronica asked.

"Two dead for sure. A lot of others wounded. They've set up emergency hospitals in the school out there. I came in here on my way to the docks."

The morning dragged by as she waited for news of loved ones. As the clock moved slowly around the circle and she heard nothing, the fear that she'd grown accustomed to turned to dread. Why hadn't her father found some way to let them know he was all right? The telephones were working and he knew where they would be. If he was back from Maui by now, he surely would have called. Had Maui been hit as well? As far as she could discover, none of the other islands had been attacked. But each hour brought a fresh rumor or firsthand account of disaster.

Some of the rumors were repeated over and over again. Nearly everyone was saying that the Japanese pilots who were shot down were wearing class rings from Honolulu's McKinley High School. Even though that rumor was officially denied, people insisted it was true.

The lines of blood donors never slowed down, and Veronica saw many of the same faces as the day before. She noticed that there were fewer Japanese faces among the donors, however, and she began to hear more and more stories about treachery from the Hawaiians of Japanese descent.

One man swore that every Japanese person on the island was a spy and they would all be locked up. "Those Jap farmers cut a big arrow in the cane fields to show the way to Pearl."

"But the planes came from the sea," Veronica protested. "They didn't need any arrows to find the harbor."

"It's there," the man insisted. "My sister's brother-in-law saw it and he's a policeman."

The rumors wore her down, and she felt more and more discouraged and tired as the afternoon wore on. Her father should have been home by now and he should have found some way to contact them. Phillip would also have found some way to contact her if he was alive, she was sure. From time to time, she called Mrs. Bennett and asked for news. The answer was always the same.

After her third call of the day, Mrs. Bennett said, "If I hear, I'll call you, my dear. Now don't call again because you may be taking up a valuable telephone line. We must remember Pearl Harbor."

That phrase, "Remember Pearl Harbor," caught on like wildfire, and by early afternoon it was on everyone's lips. People found strength in repeating the phrase to each other. It was the catchword that propelled them into additional effort when they were close to dropping from exhaustion.

Gradually, during the second day, things became more organized at the emergency blood bank, and a sense of routine replaced the feeling of emergency. Nurses who'd been working in slacks and blouses found time to change into uniforms. Those who were on vacation showed up for work.

Military orders kept coming over the radio,

but there was no news of any more bombings or attacks. People began to let go of the expectation of immediate attack and adjust to long-term terror. An attack might come at any moment, but it might not come at all.

No one could stay on alert forever. Racing blood pressure eased into fatigue, and people went about their duties with a look of grim determination.

It seemed to Veronica that people snapped at each other more, and were more difficult to work with the second day. She wasn't sure whether that was because they were more tired or less afraid. It was almost as though things were returning to normal, but beneath that apparent normalcy, fear lurked like a giant spider spinning a poisonous web that encircled them all and threatened to paralyze.

She caught fear on people's faces when they thought no one was looking. But they kept up a brave face to each other, and no one talked of defeat. Instead, they talked of a short war; of keeping up morale; and of fighting to the last man, woman, and child for their beautiful island.

Toshi came in at noon. She said, "I knew you'd worry, but my mother wouldn't let me come sooner. There's talk of rounding up all the Japanese and putting them in jail, and my mother didn't want me to go out."

"Oh, Toshi!" There didn't seem to be anything else to say.

"My brother was arrested yesterday afternoon, but they let him go after about three hours of questioning. My brother says they've taken our Buddhist priest and the Japanese language teacher to Sand Island. They've arrested some Germans and Italians, too."

"Oh, Toshi! I'm so sorry."

"We're lucky, though. My brother found out my uncle and his family are all right. Their house was bombed and my aunt was hurt, but they were lucky. The people in the house next door were all killed. They were eating breakfast when the bombs hit. All of them are dead. The Fujimotos — did you meet them?"

Toshi's face looked old, as though she'd lived a lifetime overnight. Veronica wondered if she'd aged the same way.

"Is your brother all right?"

"Yes," Toshi answered. "He wasn't even mad at the police. He just keeps saying he wants to join the American Army and help win the war. We all want to help. So I came to see if your mother would let me wash more bottles."

"Of course she will," Veronica said. Then she added, "My mother's been so brave. She's worked harder than anyone and never complained once. We haven't heard from my father yet."

"When was he supposed to be home?"

"This morning at ten. It's almost one."

"I saw Mike outside. He looked so tired, like he'd gone from sixteen to forty-five overnight."

"What's Mike doing here?"

"I'm not sure. Maybe he's helping carry wounded, because he was in the emergency room. He said he'd stop in before he left."

Veronica went with Toshi to find Annabelle. For the very first time, her mother kissed Toshi on the cheek when she saw her, and said, "I've been very worried about you. How is your family?"

"All right. My uncle's house was bombed but they're all right."

Annabelle Stewart hugged both girls close to her and said, "When I think of how close you came to getting killed. . . ."

"Look at that, she's hugging a Jap," someone said in a loud, clear voice.

They turned and saw two nurses standing and staring at the three of them. The second nurse said, "She kissed that Jap, too."

Annabelle Stewart drew herself up very tall and said in a clear voice to the nurses, "Ladies, I want you to meet my daughter's best friend, Toshi Nakamura. I've known Toshi and her family for many years, and they will continue to be my friends, despite anything you may say or do. And I will not tolerate rudeness to any volunteer worker here at this station."

The nurses glared at her, then drifted away. Veronica hugged her mother tightly to let her know how proud she was of her for standing up to them. Annabelle said in a clear, loud voice, "Now, Toshi, I want you to report any rudeness at all. I'll have Captain Stewart deal with it when he returns. Is that clear?"

"Yes, Mrs. Stewart."

In a softer voice, she said, "And Toshi, I'd like you to call your parents and ask them to be guests at my house tonight. They'll be more comfortable up on the hill, I'm sure."

"Thank you, Mrs. Stewart, but they're not afraid."

"Of course they're not afraid," Annabelle Stewart said. "None of us are afraid. But some of us need time to return to our good senses. We're all good Americans, but some foolish people may forget that. Call your family, Toshi, and issue the invitation."

"They will be honored, Mrs. Stewart." Toshi bowed politely and went to the telephone.

Annabelle watched her walk away, and said softly to Veronica, "They will be honored but they probably won't come, will they?"

"Probably not," Veronica said.

"And that will be my fault because I've never invited them before. I'm sorry, Veronica. I really am."

Veronica slipped her arm around her mother's waist and laid her head on her shoulder. "Nothing to be sorry for, Mama. You don't know how proud I am of you."

Annabelle laughed and hugged her, saying, "Won't your father be happy to see how close we've become in the last twenty-four hours?"

"Yes, he will," she agreed. But she had to fight the fear that he might not ever see it at all.

Chapter Fifteen

As the day dragged on and they didn't hear from her father, both Veronica's and Annabelle's spirits sagged. They passed each other as they went about their duties at the blood bank and tried to offer encouraging words, but they both knew that time was running out for Captain Charles Stewart's return.

They took a break together at four and Veronica suggested, "Let's go outside and get some air."

They started to walk down the long corridor, but before they'd gone thirty feet, Mike Kokohuilano came in the door. His arm was in a sling and he was limping. Both Veronica and Annabelle ran toward him. Annabelle reached him first and threw her arms around him as she asked, "What happened?"

"Got burned," Mike said. "They kicked

me off the docks, so I thought maybe you'd give me work. I can lift pretty good with my right hand. And I'm strong."

Tears ran down Annabelle's cheeks as she said, "My poor boy. My poor boy. You must go home to your mother."

"Not yet," Mike said grimly. "Not till I'm sure they're not coming back. Do you have work for me?"

"We'll find something," Annabelle promised, "but you must rest first. If you'll take an hour nap, I'll give you work."

"Nap? Where will I sleep?"

"I'll show you," Annabelle said. She was fluttering around Mike as though he were her own son.

Veronica couldn't help but smile at the about-face her mother had done in the last twenty-four hours. Was this the same woman who'd objected to Mike because he was part oriental? Who objected to Toshi because she was too foreign? Who objected to Phillip because he was a common sailor? She'd always hoped her mother's values were deeper than they appeared, and now she knew for certain that they were.

"Let's go outside first. Just for a minute," Veronica begged. "If I don't see daylight soon, I'll go crazy."

They all turned and walked out the door. The flower scents weren't as conspicuous in the daytime, but the blue sky and fresh air were paradise. Over toward the ocean the sky was still black and dark, but if she kept looking toward the mountain peaks, things looked normal. She breathed in the fresh air as though she could store it up in her lungs.

No one spoke for a long time, and then Mike began to talk. "We started working at one in the morning, just as soon as the moon came up. We pulled them in all night long. At first, they were mostly alive and some of them were holding onto broken pieces of the ship and stuff. But later, it was only bodies. And then, when dawn came, we started the rescue operations. Men came out in tugs with torches, and we cut through the metal. I swam over to the ship and heard the trapped men tapping. Tapping and tapping, and all over that ship you could hear them sending S.O.S. signals. Nobody yelled or cried, they just tapped."

"How did you get burned?" Annabelle asked.

"Accident," Mike said. "There's been a lot of accidents today. Soldiers shooting each other because they were trigger-happy. Did you know that wasn't a bombing raid last night?"

"But we heard them," Veronica protested.

"We heard our soldiers shooting down their own planes." Mike laughed shortly and said, "The Japs wanted to surprise us. They sure did. It will take months for Hawaii to recover from this. If we have months."

"Do they still think there will be an invasion of the Mainland?" Veronica asked.

"They're preparing for everything," Mike said. "There're soldiers putting up barricades all over the streets. I heard they're rounding up all the Japanese people and putting them in jail."

"That's impossible. You can't put a third of an island in jail!" Annabelle snapped. "And besides that, it's against the American constitution."

"Martial law means the military make the rules," Mike said. "And I don't mean to be critical, but the military seems pretty confused right now."

"You're tired," Annabelle said. "Come inside and I'll show you where to sleep."

"One hour," Mike cautioned.

"One hour," Annabelle promised. Then she hugged him again and said, "I just want you to know how proud I am of you and all the others who risked their lives to swim out there. I just want you to know. . . ."

"I did what I knew how to do," Mike said. "Same as you and Veronica have."

"And Toshi," Annabelle reminded them. "She's worked at the dirtiest job of all."

They let Mike sleep exactly one hour, and then Veronica woke him and asked if he'd like to take over her job. "It's pretty simple, really," she explained. "You just make sure everyone is over sixteen and under sixty, and that they haven't been sick in the last year or two. Then you hand them out juice and crackers if they have to stand in line too long. And if there's someone who has to get right back to work, you let him or her cut in front of the others."

"What do I do if I know someone is only fourteen and he tells me he's sixteen?" Mike asked. "I mean, will it hurt the plasma or just hurt the person?"

"It won't hurt the plasma," Veronica said. She was worried about Mike's burns, and she knew he must be in terrible pain. But she also understood that he wanted to help. She added, "You'll just have to use your own judgment. We're doing pretty well on blood right now. Yesterday, we were in a real panic."

"But if there's another raid tonight. . . ." Mike began.

Veronica didn't hear what he was saying because she was watching a man in a naval uniform come down the hall. The man was limping and he didn't walk a thing like her father, but when he got just a little closer she knew. She ran down the hall, calling, "Daddy! Daddy!"

Then, when she was just ten feet from him, she stopped, turned around, and ran back to her mother's station. As she ran, she called, "Mama, Mama. He's here! He's here!"

Her mother ran as fast as she could down the hall. Veronica turned again to run in the same direction, but she kept a few paces behind her mother. She stood back watching them embrace for a moment before she joined them. The joy and excitement that she felt made it very difficult for her to take in what he was actually saying.

"I got here as fast as I could. We made radio contact yesterday, but the Navy didn't send a boat for us till noon today. By the time we got here we knew that Pearl Harbor had been hit, but no one had any idea how badly until we came into the harbor." He shuddered and said, "I've got a new job. I'm to take charge of burying the dead."

"How terrible!" Annabelle said.

"Someone has to do it," he answered. Then he hugged them both and said, "I can do anything at all now that I know you're both all right."

"Will you be coming home tonight?" his wife asked.

"Not tonight," he answered. Then he frowned and said, "Maybe not for several nights, but I'll try and get home for a little while tomorrow."

"Tomorrow," Annabelle said wistfully. "Oh, Charles, do you think things will ever be normal again?"

"If the Japanese don't attack again," he began.

"But they'd be foolish not to," his wife objected. "You don't seriously expect them just to hit once and go away."

"No one knows what the Japanese will do," he answered. "No one guessed that they'd pull a surprise air raid like this. We expected them to try and attack with submarines and destroyers, if at all."

"Charles, they say that Admiral Kimmel and General Short will be court-martialed because they weren't prepared for this."

"I've heard the rumors."

"Why weren't we prepared?" Veronica asked. "Why was everyone asleep?"

"It's complicated," her father answered. "I guess it will take years to sort out all the answers to that question, but basically, we just didn't think they'd come by air. We didn't think of the ships in Pearl Harbor as targets. We thought they were protecting Hawaii and all of the Pacific from attack, not inviting it."

"I saw the second attack on Pearl," Veronica said. "The battleships were sitting targets. And earlier at Schofield, the airplanes never even got off the ground. It was terrible."

"War is always terrible." Captain Stewart looked at his watch and said, "I've got to go before I get caught in the blackout."

"How will you transport the dead at night?" Veronica asked.

"We've got the headlights painted out on the army trucks. They're all black except for a two and a half inch blue circle. We'll be able to see each other, hopefully, but no one from above will be able to spot us on the road.

"Are there many dead?" Annabelle asked.

"Yes."

"How many?"

"Too many — two thousand, maybe more. We're digging trenches at Nuuanau Cemetery and also at Red Hill. Some will get plain black boxes, but most won't."

"Daddy, my friend Phillip was on the *Arizona*."

"I'd forgotten that. I'm sorry."

"Will you see if you can find out. . . ?"

"There's not much to find out, Veronica. They're all gone."

"That can't be true," she said. Her parents didn't reply. They simply looked at her with pity in their eyes.

Chapter Sixteen

THEY camped in the hospital for a second night, and Veronica volunteered to keep watch from midnight to three.

Mike was asleep in a chair, with his head cradled in his good arm on top of the table. The burned arm lay a little to one side, and looked stiff and uncomfortable in the bandage. It was hard to think of Mike as incapacitated in any way. She was so used to seeing him move with athletic ease. Mike was the most lithe, graceful person she'd ever known, and now he was limping and holding his arm to one side as though it didn't really belong to his body. How strange that seemed.

He was in pain. She could tell that by the way he shifted and moaned in his sleep. It was strange to think of Mike in pain, stranger yet to think of Phillip as gone.

Never to see Phillip again. Was he really

dead? She didn't want to believe that, but she knew it must be so. At least two thousand young men had died during the attack. Her father was in charge of burying them, so it must be real enough. Would her father find Phillip among the many corpses that were in his charge? If he did, would he tell her? Would he even recognize him? Many of the men had been burned beyond recognition. What about Phillip? Was he lying in a communal grave already? Or had he drowned and gone to his grave in the sea?

She made no noise as she grieved for Phillip. It was her job to keep watch, not wake everyone with her emotional outbursts. She cried quietly, mindful that the sobs stayed muffled and that she did her duty.

As she cried for Phillip, she asked herself why she didn't cry for the other two thousand men as well. How could she calmly accept the casualty reports that grew ever higher, and then break down because one boy she knew was gone? Phillip seemed so special to her, but every one of those boys was special to someone. Her tears flowed, first for Phillip, and then for every man and boy who was killed and wounded during the attack.

She was sitting alone under the dim light of the only overhead lamp. She had no idea how long she sat there, but eventually she slumped and put her head in her hands, covering her tear-streaked face with her hands. It was no good trying to be brave when there was so much to cry about.

She didn't hear Mike cross the room, but she recognized his touch the minute he put his hand on her shoulder and squatted down beside her. She leaned on his shoulder, and let him circle her with his undamaged arm. As she sobbed into the warmth of his chest, he patted her on the back, soothing her as though she were a small child.

Later, when all the tears were gone, he sat beside her and held her hand. They didn't talk because there wasn't really anything to say, but she was grateful for his touch. She felt emptied of thoughts as well as tears.

There was a special kind of peace that circled around Mike and her as they sat in the dark, and she knew it was a feeling that few people are ever privileged to feel. In that instant, all she needed and wanted was satisfied by the fact that Mike was beside her. They were all alone and protected by each other's friendship. At least for the moment, Veronica felt no fear or sadness. She felt only peace.

He watched with her for the rest of her duty and at three, when she was relieved, he walked with her to the small space that was set aside as a bedroom for her, her mother, and Toshi. In the dim light, she could see that her mother was cradling Toshi in her arms, just as Mike had cradled her.

Mike hugged her and kissed her on the cheek before he helped her lie down beside her mother. She closed her eyes immediately, and fell asleep.

Chapter
Seventeen

BY Thursday, December 11, Veronica went to school, but many of the students stayed home. Her English class only had five people in it, and Mrs. Wilson, who had always been her favorite teacher, spent the whole class period talking about Japanese culture and their history of "treachery and deceit."

Veronica was glad that Toshi and the other students of Japanese descent weren't there to hear the awful things that Mrs. Wilson said.

On Friday there were even fewer students in school than on Thursday, and Veronica learned that several of them had dropped out to take jobs at the docks. Others stayed home because new rumors were circulating about a land invasion coming from the island of Maui.

For Veronica, those two days of school

165

seemed like an empty and unreal experience. Since none of her close friends were there, she found it easy to sink into a kind of stupor as she walked from class to class. The threat of impending invasion, and rumors of a massive Japanese air attack coming over the weekend, all plagued Veronica's mind and made it impossible to concentrate.

She worried a lot because her father's job was very dangerous and exhausting. Several men were badly injured in an accident because they were working too fast. She was afraid that something might also happen to her father. And she worried about Mike because he wasn't in school. His burns were a lot worse than he wanted her to know, she was sure of that. Worst of all, grief over Phillip surfaced at unpredictable moments, and tears splashed down onto her books when she least expected it.

After school on Friday, when she arrived at the hospital, her mother said to her, "I have something serious to talk to you about."

The color drained out of her face, her knees went weak, and she felt dizzy. It was an immediate and complete panic reaction, and she was so sure that her mother was going to say her father had been killed that she didn't really hear what Annabelle did say.

"So you have to help me decide what to do," Annabelle said. "It's your life that we're risking if we stay, as well as mine."

Her ears were still ringing and she asked, "Is Daddy all right?"

"Tired, that's all. But he's dead set on our going to the States. What do you think?"

"Is he coming, too?"

Annabelle stared at her in dismay. "Your father's a Navy officer. He'll stay at his post. The point is that they're evacuating families. Didn't you hear anything I said?"

"Evacuating us? Where to?"

"To California," Annabelle said. "I suppose we'd go to my sister's in South Carolina for the duration."

"Duration?"

"Duration of the war. Veronica, don't you feel well?"

"I don't want to go to South Carolina, Mama. I want to stay here, where I belong."

"It will be safer on the Mainland. A lot of people would give everything they have for a chance to board that ship. I told your father I didn't want to go but I'd talk to you."

"I don't want to go, either."

"Good girl. He'll be home tomorrow and we'll tell him. If we're both determined, we'll persuade him."

Veronica was assigned the job of sweeping the hallways. Pushing a broom didn't seem as though it was helping a lot, but Veronica knew that every little thing that people did for the war effort was important. She swept until it was almost dark and she and her mother had to take the last bus up the hill to their home.

Returning home at night was a strange

sensation because the house she'd grown up in looked so different. Instead of wide-open windows that looked out on the gardens and homes below, every window was covered with heavy back paper. "I hate all those black windows," Annabelle said. "It makes everything look so sad."

Veronica choked back the tears and said, "And curfew makes life boring. Do you think things will ever really return to normal?"

"We're on our way," Annabelle reminded her. "Your father's coming home tomorrow."

He was there when she woke the next morning. She could hear their voices getting louder and louder, and knew they were arguing over their possible evacuation to the States. Veronica slipped out of bed, wrapped her lime-green robe around her darker green pajamas, and went out on the lanai where her parents sat glaring at each other.

Neither of them looked up as she sat down at the third place at the table. She spread a napkin out on her lap and joked, "I see the war's still raging."

Her father turned to her then and smiled slowly, saying, "Hi, Ronnie. You look beautiful today. Pretty color."

She tried to smile and not let her father see how shocked she was by his face. Like so many people she was close to the last few days, he seemed to have aged twenty years overnight. He had dark circles under his eyes, and he looked thin and pale. She asked,

"Didn't they feed you at the Royal Hawaiian?"

"Royal Hawaiian?"

"We heard all the Navy officers were staying there. Didn't the military take it over two days ago?"

"Maybe so," he answered. "I've been pretty busy just doing my job. I slept last night on one of the wooden boxes we've been burying the dead in. If I hadn't been so tired, I might have crawled inside."

"Charles!"

"Sorry. I guess it really wasn't funny, but I'm at the point where it makes more sense to joke than cry."

Veronica nodded her head in agreement. "Might as well keep it light when you can. We thought you were living it up with the top brass." She wanted to ask her father if he'd heard anything about Phillip, but she was afraid that just the question would start her tears again.

"Do you think the war will last long?" she asked instead.

"If we're *lucky*, this war will last at least two years. It will take us that long to gear up enough military strength to fight the Germans and Japanese at the same time. A short war will mean only one thing, Veronica — defeat."

"You're tired, Charles," Annabelle Stewart said. "If you weren't tired, you wouldn't be talking about defeat. We'll win this war, and more quickly than you expect."

"You're not a military strategist," her husband answered in an angry voice.

"No, but I know we'll win," Annabelle flared. "You can't live through what we've lived through the last four days and not know that the American people will win this war. Charles, you should have seen the way people poured into that hospital to donate blood. Some of them didn't even know what a blood transfusion was; all they knew was that their blood was needed. They were ready to do anything to help. And your own daughter drove an ambulance."

"There's more to fighting a war than having civilians who are willing to fight."

"If you could have seen her, you would know that we're going to win. A sixteen-year-old girl who's never done a thing in her life but think about boys and clothes was ready to fight barehanded for this island. And she wasn't exceptional, she was just one of many."

"That's not the point. The point is I want you back on the Mainland where you'll be safe."

"What about all the other women and children who can't get to the Mainland? Why should we run? Shouldn't navy families set an example?" Veronica asked.

Her father shook his head and said, "Don't you two gang up on me. I know what I'm doing."

"Not this time," Annabelle Stewart said levelly.

"Mother's right," Veronica said in exactly the same voice.

Her father looked grim. Crumpling his napkin and frowning, he said, "You win. I hope you're right. And now I have to get back to work."

"When are you coming home?" his wife asked.

"I don't know," he said quietly.

Neither woman said anything as they watched him walk out.

Chapter Eighteen

LIFE took on a wartime pattern which was certainly not normal, but did have a kind of order and calm about it. Captain Stewart worked long hours during the next week, but he was able to come home nights to sleep. "The food's not as good at the Royal Hawaiian," he joked.

Not knowing when the Japanese would attack again meant that everyone lived on constant alert. The first few nights of the blackout, nervous soldiers went around shooting out stray lanterns and streetlights. By the weekend, the blackout was strictly enforced and the city of Honolulu was absolutely dark.

On Sunday afternoon, a week after Pearl Harbor, Mike came to visit, riding his bicycle with only his good arm for balance. His other arm was still bandaged. He found her sitting on the edge of the lanai, staring out at the burning ships. He sat down beside her and said, "They look kind of like daytime stars, don't they?"

"I suppose."

"Veronica, I know you're thinking about Phillip. I think about him, too, you know."

"Do you, Mike? You never even met him."

"But we had a lot in common. We were about the same age and we were in love with the same girl. It's weird to be the one who lived. Do you know what I mean?"

"It's not your fault he's gone," she said. "I know that."

"I suppose it's impossible to compete with a dead man. He'll always be the ideal hero now and I'll just be me."

He looked so handsome sitting there, she longed to turn back the clock to the days when they'd been simple teenagers on their first date. Mike had been the first one to take her to a dance, the first boy to kiss her. She sighed and said, "You'd better get going. Curfew starts in a minute."

"I came to tell you that the principal came to my house today. He wanted to know if I was coming to school tomorrow, and I said yes. I thought he was just checking up on me, but he wants me to be in charge of a new organization called the Student Defense League. The idea is to get all the high school kids ready for another attack or even a land war. Mr. Deffenbach thinks the Japs will land any day now, and he's worried about how things will go if they invade or attack during school hours. He wants everyone trained in first aid."

"I've been giving first aid lessons during lunch hour ever since Wednesday," Veronica said.

"He told me. But he wants to get every kid in school involved. He wants you and the others who know first aid to start really training the others to do something in case of war. He thinks we should be storing up emergency supplies — water and stuff."

"They're planning to use the gym for a bomb shelter. Mike, that gym is too rickety to trust."

"I think there are plans to dig other bomb shelters in the city. By the time we graduate in June, there will probably be bomb shelters in every backyard."

"Not unless we dig our own," Veronica said. "This war's only been on for a short time and there's already a labor shortage. Our cook is quitting to go to work at the Navy Yard as a cook. She's making twice what we paid her."

Mike nodded. "Anyway, I talked a long time to Mr. Deffenbach, and I promised I'd do it if you'd be my assistant."

"Then you'll stay in school." She was relieved about that. Mike had been talking about dropping out and joining the Navy.

"He convinced me I could do as much good by helping them organize the students for the war effort. And he says I can probably get into officers' training school if I hang around school long enough to graduate."

"You can be a seven-day wonder." That's what they were calling the young men who received instant promotions after the war started. As the armed forces swelled, the shortage of officers was becoming acute. Men like her father, who'd been doing desk work for years, were suddenly in charge of large groups of fighting men. Their desk jobs would be taken over by enlisted men.

"Veronica, I know you're still thinking all the time about Phillip, but I need to know if I can count on you for this job. Since you're president of the senior class and I'm student body president, Mr. Deffenbach says we're the natural leaders. He wants to close school every Friday and get all the students to work in the pineapple fields. And I said you'd train students for the Red Cross during your study hall as well as before and after school. Right?"

"Of course. It seems funny to suddenly be a teacher, but I guess I'm as well-qualified as anyone else." She smiled as she thought how proud her mother would be of her for using her Red Cross training so well. Her mother had certainly been right on that argument, and she would find a way to apologize for the fuss she'd kicked up about Red Cross meetings.

"Okay, Ronnie. We'll be together for now, and later — " He stopped himself and stood up quickly, saying, "See you tomorrow?"

"See you tomorrow, unless General Short makes a proclamation against school."

They both laughed and Mike said, "It's good to hear you joke about something."

"Bet you thought I'd stopped for the duration," she teased. "But you've got to admit he does make a lot of proclamations."

"And one of them is that I'd better get home before dark." Mike jumped on his bicycle and pedaled away.

Veronica was glad that Mike was happy she'd made a joke, but she really didn't think it was all that funny. It seemed to Veronica that General Short, who was now officially in charge of the Hawaiian Islands, must stay awake all night thinking of rules and restrictions. Grocery stores were open again but just about everything was rationed. In spite of the fact that they were sitting in the midst of the largest sugar-producing plantations on earth, sugar was rationed along with coffee, meat, and a lot of other foods.

All the bars, liquor stores, dance halls, and movies were closed, although people said he planned to open them very quickly. Curfew was strictly enforced and anyone out after six P.M. was apt to be challenged by soldiers who had nervous trigger fingers.

Military rule was probably very necessary, but it didn't make life any easier. And General Short's attitude toward civilians was not lenient. Despite complaints from local lawyers, all crimes were being tried in military courtrooms, even when the case had been on the docket long before Pearl Harbor.

The argument that people gave for turning everything over to the military was that there were too many people of Japanese descent on the island to trust a civil court system. Though most Japanese citizens were still in their homes, the threat of imprisonment remained. And many of the leaders of the Japanese community were taken without formal charges or trial and locked up on Sand Island.

Most of the Japanese newspapers were put out of business and their editors sent to Sand Island. A few were allowed to keep on printing because the military had so many new proclamations that the people had to learn about, and a large proportion of the older Japanese people couldn't read English.

Veronica sighed as she thought about all these things, and wished that life wasn't quite so complicated. She hated the Japanese who had attacked the island, and so did everyone else. But did that mean she was supposed to hate everyone whose ancestors came from Japan? It didn't make any kind of sense at all to her, but it seemed to be perfectly logical to people like Mrs. Wilson, her English teacher.

Things were so bad that Toshi had only come to school one day last week. When the other students taunted her, she held her head up high, but she hadn't returned. Now, as Veronica watched the *Arizona* blaze in the dying light, she promised herself that she would do everything she possibly could to defeat the Japanese, but she would never abandon her friends just because they happened to have Japanese ancestors.

The next morning, when she went to school, Toshi was in her first period class. Veronica asked, "Why didn't you wait for me at the bottom of the stairs like you always do?"

Toshi just smiled and said, "Good to see you, Veronica."

They talked for a few minutes and then class began. On their way out, Veronica said, "Will you help Mike and me with the defense committee we're starting? Can you come to the planning meeting at lunch?"

"Are you sure you want me?" Toshi asked.

"Yes, I'm sure," Veronica replied. "And if there's anyone there who doesn't, we'll just tell them to go away."

No one actually objected when Toshi and three other students of Japanese descent showed up at the meeting. There were a few rude stares but Mike put an end to that very quickly by saying, "I've been asked to be chair of this group because I'm student body president. Veronica is co-chair because she's senior class president. We've appointed Toshi Nakamura as secretary. Any objections?"

Mike glared at the few students who might have objected, and they held their silence. The meeting got underway, and very quickly they had a plan for student activities that pleased most of the people there. Mike ended the meeting by saying, "Then we've agreed to give one school day a week to the pineapple fields. And we'll have Red Cross training sessions until Veronica and the others have trained at least two hundred students. Right?"

Only one boy objected. He said, "I don't see why we should have to work for free when other people are getting paid big money."

"We're working for democracy," Mike answered.

"Seems to me we're working for the plantation owners," the student said. "I'd rather get a job down at the docks. They're paying a dollar an hour, I hear."

"If you go to work at the docks, you don't finish school," Veronica said.

"So what?"

"So America needs educated people. . . ." Veronica began, but the young man turned away, obviously uninterested.

"Let him go," Mike said. "We've got too much work to do to worry about one bum apple."

"Who's calling me a bum apple?"

Mike simply ignored him and started assigning emergency posts to various students. When he gave Toshi the job of standing by the school office in case of attack, another student objected.

"That's a really important job. Do we want a Jap doing it?"

"I'm the chair and I assigned Toshi Nakamura. John, you think you can handle the stretcher room? I'll give you a couple of strong helpers."

After the meeting, Toshi and Veronica walked out with Mike. Toshi said, "Thank you, Mike. I appreciate what you did."

"I did my job," he answered.

"You were willing to stick your neck out," Veronica said, "It's all right to take a little credit."

"No credit due," Mike answered shortly.

"Yes there is," Toshi said. "You have no idea what we're going through and how people are treating us. Did you know that they won't let our young men join the Army? Can you imagine what it feels like to want to fight for your country and not be allowed to? At least you gave me a chance to be useful, Mike."

"You may not thank me after a few days in the pineapple fields," Mike joked. "It's a lot tougher to cultivate pineapple than to translate Latin."

"I'll do a lot more than that to prove that I'm a good American," Toshi said. "So will the rest of us Japanese Hawaiians." Toshi's prediction proved to be correct. In the next few days, many more Japanese students reappeared at school and volunteered their time and work to the student committee. No job was too tough for them, and they never complained about anything.

A group of older students from all over the city organized a separate group called

180

the Varsity Victory Volunteers. They had older men from the Japanese community as leaders, and they drafted a letter to the military governor and commanding general of the army. The letter said, "Hawaii is our home, the United States is our country. We know but one loyalty, and that is to the stars and stripes. We wish to do our part as loyal Americans in every way possible and we hereby offer ourselves for whatever service you see fit."

The Varsity Victory Volunteers were assigned to the Army Corps of Engineers, and they worked harder than anyone at digging ditches, building barracks, making roads, and doing any other kind of war work that they could get.

As people settled into the new wartime routines, the truth about what happened those first few days gradually emerged. They learned that over two thousand Americans were killed and more than a thousand were wounded. Most of the casualties were sailors and soldiers, but there had been more than two hundred civilians killed.

Chapter Nineteen

THERE were almost no Christmas trees in Hawaii that year. Sixty thousand trees were sent from Washington, but they were lost on the *Mauna Ala* when she sank. Some people used small potted palms, and others bought the few artificial trees that were available in the stores. The Stewarts voted to have no Christmas tree at all but to celebrate the holiday simply by going to church.

Nothing about the holiday seemed the same that year. The outdoor decorations that usually lit up the downtown section of Honolulu were banned because of the blackout. If people had Christmas lights inside their homes, they were only for private enjoyment; the heavy black paper of the blackout kept anyone else from seeing them.

Veronica spent the three days of vacation before Christmas volunteering at the hospital. Though the emergency was over for the moment, there was plenty of work to do. Many of the women who were volunteers during the Pear Harbor emergency were already working in defense jobs. No one questioned that more women would begin working just as soon as the United States geared up its factories and shipyards for full production.

Veronica was constantly surprised at how Pearl Harbor had changed people. Her mother was more relaxed, more loving, and much more tolerant than she'd been before. It was as if the bombs that dropped had shaken up her values and let her see what was really important. The one thing that Veronica could honestly say she was grateful for on that Christmas morning was the change in her mother. And the change in her relationship with her mother, she reminded herself.

She wondered if she had changed as much as other people had. She supposed she was more serious and more responsible than she might have been without the war. And, in a way, she liked herself better now that she knew she was a brave person. Seeing yourself behave well in an emergency built self-esteem.

Not everyone had changed for the better, of course. Her English teacher got more unpleasant each day. She seemed absolutely incapable of talking about anything but the war and how she hated the Japanese. There was a rumor that she planned to join the Women's Army Auxiliary Corps that they were talking about establishing. That would mean a substitute teacher for the remainder of the year, but everyone would be relieved to see her go.

Christmas dinner was simple, and Veronica couldn't help comparing it to the feast they'd had at Thanksgiving. About halfway through the meal, Annabelle Stewart looked up and said, "Do you remember how that boy liked my pie? Didn't he have two pieces?"

Instead of bursting into tears and running from the room, Veronica smiled at her mother and said, "Yes. He said it was the best dinner he'd ever had."

"Did he really?" There were tears running down her mother's face.

"Yes, it was good pie," Veronica said. Then she left the table and went to her room, where she threw herself on the bed and let the tears flow freely.

Later, her father knocked on the door and asked for permission to come in. He sat on the edge of her bed and patted her shoulder as he said, "Your mother shouldn't have upset you like that. She's sorry. It's just that she's very upset herself today."

Veronica knew what was coming next. She turned to face her father and asked, "When do you leave?"

"I'm not sure. The transfer came through yesterday. I can't tell you any more."

"A slip of the lip sinks the ship," Veronica

repeated. It was one of the slogans that people used to remind themselves not to talk about anything that the enemy might want to know.

"I'll be leaving soon, Ronnie. I want you to know that I asked for active duty. I almost didn't get it because of my age, but there's a shortage of officers so I persuaded the top brass to let me go."

"When will you be back?"

"I don't know. That's one of the things about living through a war that you and your mother will just have to get used to — the uncertainty. You know the Navy. I may not leave for months, and then again, I may be gone by tomorrow morning."

"Yes." She threw her arms around her father and sobbed. He held her close and smoothed her hair as he talked to her. "You'll have to help your mother, Ronnie. You know that."

"We'll be fine." The words were muffled by her sobs but she knew he heard them.

"I know you will. You're both brave girls and I'm proud of you. Now put on your prettiest dress and we'll all go for a walk in the park."

"What park?" Veronica asked.

"I thought we might just take the bus down to the Foster Gardens," he said.

"Not there," Veronica pleaded. "That's where Phillip took me on our first date."

"Then somewhere else," her father agreed quickly. "But Ronnie, you've got to try and get over your grief about Phillip as soon as you can. You're young, you have everything to live for."

She didn't say what she was thinking — that Phillip had also been young and had also had everything to live for. She just nodded her head and said, "I'm all right as long as I'm working. Did mother tell you I want to leave school?"

"Yes, and we can't permit it. However, we did agree that if you will finish high school on schedule, we'll let you delay college for the duration."

"But I feel so foolish in school while everyone else is working for the war effort. I know that I could do something to help. I could learn to weld, I could build ships. Other women are doing that."

"A high school education is absolutely essential. You can volunteer as much as you want, as long as you keep your grades up."

"I just don't feel that I'm doing enough."

"You're doing plenty," he said. "And in June, if you choose, you can do something different. Promise me you'll finish high school, Veronica. If you possibly can."

She gave him her reluctant promise and then the three of them took the bus to downtown Honolulu for a walk along Waikiki Beach. Everything seemed changed because the hotels were now military headquarters and the streets were filled with young men in sailor suits and other military uniforms.

They all tried their best to enjoy the afternoon; Veronica knew the Stewart family was trying to make a memory that would stay with them for the duration of the war. They found that several of the tourist shops were open even though it was Christmas Day, and her father said, "Let's go in. I want to buy you both a present."

Annabelle laughed and said, "I just opened my Christmas presents a few hours ago."

"This is different," he assured her. "This is a New Year's present." He picked out a thin silver bracelet for his wife and slipped it over her wrist. He bought two silver barrettes for Veronica. They were shaped like butterflies. "When you wear these you can think of me," he said. Then he hugged them both and asked, "Anyone ready for Chinese food?"

"We just ate Christmas dinner," they both objected.

"Christmas dinner isn't Christmas dinner without a little chop suey for dessert," he assured them.

Later, they took the last bus back and were at their corner before curfew. They planned to go home and listen to music on their gramophone, but as they started down the block toward their house, Mr. Bennett called out to them. He invited them in for a drink, saying, "You can get home all right," he said. "There's some moon tonight."

Veronica hated to go to the Bennetts' because she knew that it would remind her of the first time she'd met Phillip. She said, "I'll go on home."

"No," her father said. "Stay with us tonight, Ronnie. I don't want you to be alone."

And so they went to the Bennetts' and had a glass of sherry together. Mr. Stewart proposed a toast, "To our godson, Phillip Easterwood, who gave his life for us."

Solemnly, they all drank their sherry and the Stewarts rose to go home. Veronica held her mother's hand in the darkness of the blackout, and her father went ahead, as though to protect them from danger. But neither her father nor anyone else could protect them from what was to come.

That night, as Veronica lay in bed, she looked up at her ceiling and wished she could look out at the stars as she'd done before her windows were blacked out. The tears were all gone now and she stared dry-eyed at the future. Would the war really take three or four years? Would Hawaii be invaded? And would the time ever come again when things were normal? It was only three weeks since the war began, but she'd almost forgotten what peacetime felt like.

Chapter Twenty

HER father didn't really say good-bye. He simply didn't come home on the twenty-seventh, and they knew he was gone. Annabelle Stewart said little, but Veronica knew that she took his departure very hard because her eyes were so red and swollen the next morning that she had to wear dark glasses to the hospital.

Like Veronica, Annabelle Stewart clearly needed work to keep her from sinking into depression, and she told her daughter that night that she planned to work twelve hours a day for a while. "We're shorter of personnel that ever," she said. "And they've asked me to take charge of all the volunteer activities."

"That's a real promotion," Veronica said.

"Promotion by default," Annabelle answered. "I'm one of the ones who's sticking with Red Cross volunteer work. A lot of the others are going into paying jobs. You can't blame them, of course."

"Some people will get rich and other people will get killed," Veronica said.

"It isn't like you to be bitter," Annabelle corrected gently. "You were always such a cheerful girl."

They spent New Year's Eve at the hospital, each volunteering for extra duty since the holiday depleted the work force even more. On New Year's Day, they were back at their posts by early in the afternoon, in time to hear the first news about the second attack on Hawaii.

The news come in pieces, partly by radio, partly by newspaper, and mostly by word of mouth, but by the end of the day they knew pretty well what had happened. A Japanese submarine was seen off the cliffs of Hamakua Coast on the island of Hawaii. And residents of Hilo were wakened at midnight when the submarines shelled the large oil storage tanks on the waterfront. At first it was said that many people were killed, but later reports said no one was hurt.

Later, they learned that submarines had also attacked the island ports of Kahului, Maui, Nawailiwili, and Kauai. It was a well-organized and widespread attack, and it frightened residents of the islands even more than they had been before. Talk of locking up all the Japanese Hawaiians started again, and people stopped complaining about martial law.

Veronica went back to school after New Year's Day, and she and Mike threw themselves into training the Student Defense League. Not only did Veronica head up the group of volunteers who taught first aid, but she worked with Mike organizing the work days on the plantations.

She and Mike shared the same frustration about not doing enough for the war effort, and they spurred each other on to greater efforts. Neither of them paid much attention to school subjects, but their teachers seemed willing to overlook their absences since they were doing so much for the war effort.

Veronica was proudest on the days when they closed school and everyone went to the pineapple fields to work.

One day when they were working together in the fields, Mike and she were eating lunch together. He took her hand and said, "It's good to have you back."

"Have I been gone?"

"Sort of. But the color's back in your cheeks and you're full of the old Ronnie."

"I'm trying," Veronica admitted. She did feel better and that seemed so sad. Phillip had been dead just a few weeks.

Mike took her hand and said, "Ronnie, I want you to be my girl again."

"Not yet," she answered. "It's not right."

"You weren't engaged to him," Mike said. "He was just a boy you dated a few times."

"I can't explain it," Veronica said. "All I can do is tell you it's still too early."

"Then I'll wait," Mike said softly, and Veronica sighed, knowing he meant it.

February came and went without incident, and also without word from Captain Stewart. Then, on March 1st, he walked in the front door about six o'clock in the morning. Her mother was still in bed but Veronica was up, making the coffee. She dropped a cup, she was so startled, and then ran to throw her arms around him.

He hugged her and said, "I'm here for just a few minutes. I can't tell you where I've been or where I'm going, but I can tell you that I will leave at eleven o'clock this morning."

"So soon?"

"Yes. So soon," he sat down at the kitchen table and asked, "Now how about fixing your old father a nice breakfast?"

"I should wake Mama."

"In a minute. How's she doing, Ronnie?"

"Fine, Daddy. Really fine. She's working too hard, but she's really fine."

"Start scrambling those eggs," he ordered. "I'm starved. And what about you? Things going all right?"

"I'm working hard, too. Mike and I are in charge of all the war effort activities at the school. I'm due at the pineapple field today. We close school one day a week and work in the fields. Did you get my letters?"

"One."

"I've written you every week." She wondered where her father had been and why he looked so gray and tired. There were deep, dark circles under his eyes, as though he was permanently going without sleep.

"Tell me what the letters said, Ronnie."

He seemed to want to hear the sound of her voice, so she fixed him breakfast and chattered about her activities. She deliberately tried to keep her conversation as light and easy as she could. As she worked and talked, her father watched her every move, as though he was hungry for the sight of her.

When she put the eggs down in front of him, she said, "I'll wake Mama now. If I don't she'll never speak to me again."

When she saw the look in her mother's and father's faces as they greeted each other, Veronica decided to leave for the pineapple fields. Though it nearly killed her to leave her father any earlier than she had to, she knew her parents wanted to spend some of the precious minutes they had together alone.

She kissed them both good-bye and went out the door with tears in her eyes. She was sorry to leave her father, of course, but she was also thinking of herself. Would she ever feel the same kind of love for anyone that her mother and father felt for each other?

Chapter
Twenty-one

ON March 4th, at two o'clock in the morning, Veronica was wakened by a terrific explosion. She jumped out of bed and ran to her mother's room as a second, third, and fourth explosion rocked the air. The ground seemed to tremble and she was sure that the Japanese were landing.

When she got to her mother's room, Annabelle was already up and dressing. They exchanged a few quick words and Veronica ran back to her room to get into her clothes. Then the two of them got into the car and started down the hill toward the hospital.

The sirens wailed but there were no more explosions. Since Veronica was driving in the dark, it took all her concentration just to keep the car on the road, but as they pulled into the parking lot of the hospital, Annabelle said, "It may not be a full-scale attack after all."

"Maybe not," Veronica agreed. Her heart was still racing and she felt just as excited and frightened as she'd felt the day Pearl Harbor was attacked. It was hard for her to adjust to the fact that there were no more bombs falling and there were no planes flying overhead.

They reported for duty at the hospital, but there were no emergency wounded to care for. Though they went through the motions of setting up the emergency blood bank again, by the time things were in place it was apparent that there was not going to be a real attack at all. Annabelle said, "Let's get a cup of coffee before we take everything down again."

In the cafeteria, they learned what had happened. One lone plane flew over Hawaii and dropped four bombs. No other planes followed. The volunteers stood around in worried clusters till it became apparent that nothing more was going to happen, then they were dismissed. Since it was almost dawn when they were dismissed, Veronica and Annabelle decided to wait and drive home in the daylight. On their way, they went to look at the large bomb craters that had landed near Roosevelt High School.

Veronica shuddered as she thought of what kind of damage those bombs might have done during the school day. For the first time, the total realization of what sort of responsibility she had as co-chair of the Student Defense League really hit her.

Veronica was glad it was a Saturday because she would have a chance to get some sleep before she kept her date with Mike at two. She and her mother drove home in silence, partly because they were both so sleepy and partly because they were still shaken by what those explosions might have meant to the Island. Living with the fear of invasion was wearing everyone down and it was hard to see when the terror would be lifted.

Veronica saw the young man sitting on the lanai before she pulled the car into the garage, but she just thought he was some sailor who'd wandered too far from base the night before. It was only after she parked the car and walked closer that it dawned on her who it was.

Even then, she doubted her eyes and when she first said, "Phillip?" it was a question. When she realized she was really looking at Phillip, she was so shocked that she stopped absolutely still and stared at him.

He smiled and held his arms open wide, stepping forward to embrace her. She took in the fact that he was limping and that he had the dark circles under his eyes that most servicemen had. Then she closed her eyes and fell into his arms. They kissed and hugged and held each other close for a long time before they talked.

Then it was Annabelle who asked the questions. Veronica was still too stunned and excited to think straight. She kept saying over and over again, "We thought you were dead."

"I was on the *Arizona* when we were bombed, but I was picked up by a destroyer right away," he explained.

"All the others were killed," Annabelle said. "It was almost a total loss."

"So I understand," Phillip said gravely. "But I was lucky. I was blown overboard by the first bomb and thrown clear of most of the explosion. I wasn't even hurt."

"But you're limping," Annabelle said.

"I got that at Wake Island," Phillip said. "In some ways, that battle was a lot worse than Pearl Harbor. That time we knew what was happening but we couldn't do much. A lot of us still think we could have saved the island if Admiral Pye hadn't ordered us to withdraw."

"Why didn't you write?" Annabelle asked.

Phillip looked away quickly, and then said, "I did."

"We thought you were dead," Veronica said again. She was still having trouble believing what she knew was true. And Phillip seemed very different, too. She'd thought about him so much, it was almost as though this young man standing here on the lanai was a different Phillip than the one she remembered.

"Wake Island fell in December," Annabelle protested. "And you were wounded. They should have. . . ." Her words trailed off. It was foolish to think that a ship would return to port just to deposit the wounded.

"After Wake Island, the destroyer went to the Philippines. We fought a lot but I was out of it most of the time. My leg wound was so infected they thought they might have to amputate. But I was lucky. It got better."

"Is that why you didn't let us know you were alive?" Annabelle asked. "You thought you might lose your leg?"

When Phillip didn't answer, she knew that must be the reason. Veronica felt a quick flash of anger. Why hadn't he trusted her enough to write and tell the truth?

"And when did you get back?" Annabelle asked.

Phillip's answer was a quick laugh. "About an hour ago. I hightailed it up here as fast as I could. Guess I'd better go let the Bennetts know the bad penny has returned."

"The Bennetts don't know?" Veronica asked.

"I wanted to see you first," Phillip said. He reached over to her and pulled her close, kissing her on the lips and then saying, "Sunny, I thought about you all the time. Even when I was floating around in that water with the burning oil coming at me, your face was in front of me. And during the Wake Island massacre. . . . It was awful, Sunny, but you were always there with me."

Veronica smiled and let Phillip kiss her again and again. He seemed to need to touch her and hold her, to know that she was real. And she was so happy to have him home again that it seemed perfectly natural to walk to the Bennetts' house, arm in arm.

They still had their arms around each other later in the day when Mike came riding up on his bicycle. He was obviously startled to see Veronica with a sailor and he said, "Ronnie, are you ready to go?"

She'd forgotten that they had plans to go out to the pineapple plantation together to chart the next phase of the work. "Mike, this is Phillip Easterwood," she said gently.

Mike had the presence to shake hands with Phillip and say, "Congratulations. How did you get out alive?"

Veronica could see by the stiff way that Mike held himself that he was not only shocked, he was terribly upset that she was standing with her arm around Phillip. She wanted to move apart from him but it seemed as though that would be a cruel thing to do. After all, Phillip was so very glad to see her that it would probably hurt him to have her show any signs of discomfort while Mike was there.

She let Phillip keep his arm around her possessively as he told Mike all about the battles on Wake Island and the Philippines. She could hardly bear to look at Mike's face. It was tight and drawn, as he tried to mask his emotions. She could tell just by the stiffness in his posture and the correctness of his questions that he was dying of jealousy.

Poor Mike. She knew him well enough to know that he would feel bad about being jealous. She also knew that Mike was a nice person and a patriot. He would be glad that another serviceman had been saved.

After a few minutes, she asked him, "Do you want to take the car out to the fields alone?"

"Then you're not coming?"

"Not today."

"I've got the rest of the week off," Phillip said, and hugged Veronica closer to him. "Sunny's going to show me the rest of the Island. She's the best tour guide in the world." Then he kissed her on the cheek and smiled at Mike.

Veronica was surprised that Phillip couldn't see what kind of pain Mike was in, but she supposed it was natural for a man who'd been at war as long as he had to think primarily of himself.

All Mike said was, "Have a good time."

"Don't you want to take the car?"

"I can go on my bike if I'm alone."

"But that's a long way to ride, and your arm isn't really healed." She turned to Phillip and said, "Mike was wounded when he swam out into the burning water to save sailors."

"That so?" Phillip asked.

"Have fun," Mike said, and he turned and rode away on his bicycle. Veronica's eyes followed him until he was down the hill and out of sight. Then she turned back to Phillip and asked, "What do you want to do?"

"Everything," Phillip said. "I want to walk in the gardens. Go to the beach. Eat Chinese food and pineapple. Go swimming. Everything."

Veronica laughed and said, "We'll do what we can in two days. But you have to report back to ship on Monday, and I have to go to school."

"I'm stationed in Hawaii for the duration," Phillip said. "I've got a desk job now on account of my wounded leg. Isn't that something to celebrate?"

"Yes," Veronica said, "it certainly is."

"So let's celebrate," Phillip said, linking his arm through hers. "Do you think we can use the car?"

"We're supposed to conserve on gasoline," Veronica said doubtfully.

"But don't you think a returning war hero deserves at least one tank of extra gas?"

"Half a tank," Veronica answered with a laugh. "That's all there is."

Chapter Twenty-two

NOW that Phillip was back, Veronica felt as if she'd been tied up in knots for months and someone had come along and cut through the biggest rope. As they drove home on Sunday night, she said, "If only I knew for certain that my father was safe, I'd be totally and completely happy tonight."

Phillip slipped his arm around her and said, "I'm here now. I'll take care of you."

"That's not what I mean," Veronica said quickly. "In a way, the war's been good for mother and me both. We've learned we can take pretty good care of ourselves. I'll bet a lot of women are learning the same thing. But I miss my father and I love him. I want him safe because I love him."

"And you love me," Phillip said, and nuzzled her neck.

Veronica had to be careful not to be angry

with Phillip for not understanding what she was saying any better. She knew that if she'd been talking with Mike, he would have understood her perfectly. But Mike and she were longtime friends and a great team, so it wasn't fair to compare Phillip to him. Phillip was fun to be with, but their two days together had shown her how much they still had to learn about each other.

After they parked the car, Phillip slipped his arm around her and said, "We can get married right away now that I know I have a desk job. I wouldn't ask you if I thought there was any danger I'd be shipping out again. You're too young to wait alone, but I'm going to be right here for the rest of the war. They almost as much as promised me that."

"I'm not ready to get married," Veronica said. Her heart was beating wildly and she wanted to get out of the car. She didn't want to have Phillip disappointed or upset on his first weekend home, but she wasn't going to marry him or anyone else for a long time.

"You're my girl," Phillip said, and he kissed her possessively. "We'll talk about it again."

"I've got to go now. Curfew starts in a few minutes."

"Sure it does, but I don't have very far to travel. I'm staying all night at the Bennetts'."

They held hands as they walked into her house. Annabelle greeted them with a worried frown and she said, "Veronica, I want to talk to you alone."

"Is it Daddy?" Veronica's voice faltered.

"No," Annabelle said. Then she turned to Phillip and said, "I think you should spend some of your time with the Bennetts. They're very fond of you, you know."

"I'd rather stay here," Phillip said.

"Then please excuse us for a moment." Annabelle's voice was sharp and Veronica realized she hadn't heard that particular tone for a long time.

The minute Phillip stepped outside onto the lanai, Annabelle said, "Mike came by to say good-bye. He joined the Navy."

"No!"

"I tried to get him to at least wait until you got home, but he said he'd been thinking about it for a long time. I told him not to do anything foolish, that you weren't really serious about Phillip, but he said that wasn't the reason he was leaving."

"Where is he? I've got to stop him!"

"He left about noon today. By now he's on a bus on his way to the training center."

Veronica's mind was racing wildly; she reached out for the only hope she could find. "Maybe they won't take him. Maybe they'll turn him down because of that burned arm."

"The arm's healed, Veronica. He said he'd planned all along to go when it was better."

"He planned to go when he graduated, not before," Veronica said. "He's joined now because of Phillip." She turned to her mother and said, "You told me once that I shouldn't let this war make me bitter. But I ask you how I'm supposed to keep from feeling bitter about this? I get one of them back today, and lose the other one. And if Mike is killed or wounded, it will be my fault."

"Nonsense," Annabelle said. "Mike knows what he's doing and his parents signed his enlistment papers. You're no more at fault for that than you are responsible for Phillip's happiness."

"That's what I mean," Veronica said. "I feel like it's all up to me."

Mike sent her a letter a week later and he said the same thing her mother said. "Don't think I joined because my heart was broken. I planned it all along. Just make sure you keep up the good work at the Student Defense League, and don't do anything foolish. I hope you write."

She did write to Mike, of course. And she tried to keep her letters cheerful and lighthearted because she knew that letters from home were important. She sometimes mentioned Phillip in her letters because she felt it was important to let Mike know the truth. On the other hand, she never mentioned Mike to Phillip because she felt it would distress him.

She didn't see as much of Phillip as they had expected during the next few months because they were both so busy. Veronica was determined to fulfill her responsibilities at the hospital and school, and Phillip's job turned out to be a lot more demanding than he'd believed. "They promised me a desk job and I thought they meant nine to five, but they really meant I'd be chained to the desk fourteen or more hours a day."

When they did get together they had fun, except that Phillip still asked her to marry him every time they saw each other, and then got annoyed when she refused. He seem to have a hard time understanding her determination to finish high school before she made any sort of commitment. She used a lot of different reasons to put him off, including her mother's objections, but she never told him the truth. The truth was too awkward and embarrassing. The plain fact of the matter was that the minute Phillip came back and Mike left, she realized that it was Mike she'd loved all along.

Instead of confronting the issue, she allowed things to jog along, hoping that something would happen to make everything work out of its own accord. One day she told Toshi what she was really feeling, and added, "I think we had a conversation a lot like this the week before they bombed Pearl Harbor. It's not exactly funny, is it? Look how everything has changed so much and I'm still in the same stupid place."

"Not true," Toshi said crisply. Since Mike's departure, Veronica was chair of the Student Defense League and she was co-chair. The job had earned her the respect and acceptance of most of the students, and Toshi seemed much more at ease these last few weeks. "There's a big difference, if you'll remember. You didn't know which one you liked best on December sixth. Now you tell me you know it's Mike."

"It's Mike, all right," Veronica said. "And I feel like such a hypocrite letting Phillip kiss me. He thinks we're going to get married some day. I feel like Suzie Chu."

Toshi laughed at the idea. Suzie Chu was a silly little tenth grader who met a different sailor each weekend and fell madly in love with each one. She bragged about how many different sailors she was writing to. They said she kept a battle map pinned on the wall of her bedroom, and had pins all over the world that represented boyfriends.

"I wonder what Suzie will do when the war's over and they all show up on her doorstep?" Toshi asked.

"Throw a party," Veronica answered. "Maybe I should try to be more like Suzie and not worry so much."

"Sounds like a good idea," Toshi said. "What are we going to do about the new bomb shelters?"

"Dig them, I guess. I said we could probably get some kids together on Saturdays and do the heavy work. What do you think?"

They talked only about the war effort and

their job for the rest of the day, but when they left school, Toshi said, "If I were you, I'd write to Mike and tell him how I felt. And I'd start letting Phillip down gently."

"I think I would have done that sooner if it hadn't felt unpatriotic," Veronica confessed. Then she sighed and said, "I'm not sure I can let Phillip down gently. He's kind of opinionated, you know."

But she did write to Mike in her next letter and she closed it with a hint of the truth. "I feel very foolish saying this, but ever since you left I realized how much you mean to me."

That weekend, she said to Phillip, "I think you might like to start dating some other girls."

"That's a stupid thing to say."

"All right," Veronica said. "I'll say it in a different way. I don't think I'm in love with you. I think I might be in love with Mike."

"Mike?"

"The boy you met the day you came home."

"That kid?"

"He's a few months younger than you. He's in the Navy now, same as you are."

"You're just feeling war nerves," Phillip said. "You'll get over that when these air raid sirens stop."

"They do drive me crazy," Veronica admitted. During the last few weeks they'd had an air raid alert nearly every day, but there had been no more attacks. Though most people still dropped everything and went to the bomb shelters, others were refusing to stop their lives for false alarms.

"They drive everyone crazy," Phillip said. "So just give me a kiss and let's forget about the war for a while."

Chapter
Twenty-three

Somehow, her father found a way to get home for her high school graduation. He arrived the morning before and said he could only stay for three days. "They'll fly me back to the ship," he said.

It was the first indication they'd had that he was on an aircraft carrier, and she didn't ask him anything else. It seemed strange not to know any more than she did about what the men in her life were actually doing. All she knew about Mike was that he was somewhere in the Atlantic Ocean. And even Phillip's desk job was secret.

It was easy to stick to safe subjects when her father returned, though, because there was so much to say to each other. By the time they'd recounted Phillip's miraculous return and Mike's departure, it felt as though they'd always been sitting around the breakfast table together.

Annabelle Stewart reached over and put her hand over her husband's, saying, "You'll never know how we miss you."

"I was beginning to wonder," he joked. "You two seem to be getting along so well. Next time I come home, I expect you both to be dressed like Rosie the Riveter."

He was referring to a cartoon character they were using on a lot of posters, showing a muscular woman in overalls who worked as a welder. So many women were going into defense work that Rosie the Riveter was a way of symbolizing all of them.

Annabelle and Veronica looked at each other significantly. He asked, "Okay. Which one of you gets to tell me?

"Tell you what?" Annabelle asked.

"Tell me whatever you're both making high signs to each other about. You're not thinking of marrying that boy, are you?"

"No, Daddy. I'm not."

"Good."

"I'm going to go to work at the hospital as a student nurse," she said.

"They're starting a new training program," Annabelle interjected. "They'll train you while you work, and in six months, you'll be a full-fledged nurse."

"I don't know," Captain Stewart said doubtfully. "Nursing's hard work, and I always thought you'd be a school teacher if you worked at all. Why can't you just stay home with your mother?"

"Mother's never home," Veronica answered. "Don't you know she's working harder than anyone at the hospital?"

"But volunteer work is — "

"Volunteer work is unpaid, Charles, that's the only difference." Annabelle dipped her spoon into her coffee and stirred for a moment before she added, "I'm planning to take the nurses' training, also."

"Nonsense!"

"It isn't nonsense, Daddy. Mother will be a good nurse and there's a real need for older women."

"I'm not going to talk about this idiotic idea anymore," he said. "No wife of mine —"

Annabelle stood up abruptly; her face was tight and she held her lips in a grim line. She said, "Charles, you'll only be here three days and we don't want to quarrel, so don't make any pronouncements you can't enforce. Now let's go see Veronica graduate."

The ceremony was very short. Mr. Deffenbach talked about the boys who weren't able to be at their own graduation because they were fighting in the war. Then he read a list of those on active service and the three young men from their high school who were already dead. Veronica's heart rose in her throat all the way through the service as she thought about the changes that she'd lived through this senior year.

When the ceremony started, she missed Mike so much that tears rose to her eyes, and her throat tightened to keep back the sobs. But then a strange thing happened all of a sudden: She had a very strong sense of peace and the feeling that Mike was with her in spirit. She could almost feel him beside her; she imagined his tall, broad-shouldered body next to hers. She closed her eyes and saw his wide smile and his teeth flashing in the Hawaiian sunshine. She saw the way his eyes seemed to flicker and change colors, and she heard his laughter.

The feeling that he was standing right there beside her was so strong that she jumped when the principal read his name as one of the boys who was fighting for his country. She wondered where Mike was that very minute and hoped that he was safe. He might even be thinking about the graduation and wishing that he were with them. That might be why she felt his presence so strongly.

Toshi's valedictorian speech was short and to the point. It was all about the determination of all Americans to win the war. When she finished, a few people in the audience sat silently and refused to clap for anyone of Japanese descent, but most of the students, teachers, and parents clapped long and loudly.

There was almost never any talk about locking up all the Hawaiian Japanese anymore, but they were doing exactly that in California. On President Roosevelt's order, they were being herded into trucks and taken to remote inland camps where they would be expected to stay for the duration. Despite this harsh treatment, young men of Japanese descent were still clamoring loudly for a chance to fight the enemy, and there was talk of forming an all-Japanese battalion to fight in Europe.

Annabelle and Charles Stewart made a point of sitting next to Mr. and Mrs. Nakamura at the graduation, and later at the senior tea. Veronica had never seen her mother as gracious and friendly as she was to Toshi's parents that day.

Like most Hawaiians, the Stewarts were genuinely shocked by the action taken on the Mainland against the people of Japanese descent. While some cynics said the same thing might have happened in Hawaii if there hadn't been so many Japanese, most people thought that in the long run the racial tolerance in Hawaii would have prevented such action.

The sun shone all day long and Veronica thought everyone looked handsome and beautiful, even though no one had new clothes for graduation day. She was wearing the same yellow dimity dress that she'd been wearing when she met Phillip six months ago, although now it was a little tight. She hadn't put on any weight, but she was taller and broader in the shoulders. All that heavy work in the hospital was giving her muscles.

Phillip came to the graduation exercises, of course. Though she'd done her best to persuade him that she wasn't serious about him, he persisted in talking about their future together. After the ceremony, he asked, "Will you marry me now?"

"No, Phillip."

"Why not? You're out of high school."

"I'm not going to marry you," she said for what seemed to be the hundredth time. She called to Toshi and Lana Achun, who were talking together. "Come over here and talk to us."

Phillip seemed annoyed that she wanted to introduce him to anyone else. He knew it was a way to turn the conversation, and he was barely friendly until Lana looked at him with laughter in her face and asked, "Why are you so sad on such a happy day?"

Lana looked especially happy that day. Her broad cheekbones and slanted eyes made her the kind of Hawaiian beauty that everyone wanted to put on postcards. She was wearing a pretty pink dress with puffed sleeves, and she had on short white gloves.

Phillip smiled and answered, "I'm trying to persuade Veronica what a fine catch I am, but she isn't interested."

"Then perhaps she's foolish," Lana said. "What kind of a fish are you?"

"Fish?"

"That's what we call catch here in the Islands. Are you a cold fish like most Mainlanders?"

Phillip blinked and then realized that Lana was flirting with him. He smiled and answered her, "You may not know it, but I'm a Hawaiian, too."

She laughed aloud at that. "All you handsome sailors will go home when the war's over, and we'll be very lonely."

"This is my home," he pronounced. "I'm staying."

He hardly noticed as Toshi and Veronica drifted away to speak to some other students. There was no yearbook to sign because there was a paper shortage, and what little paper could be had on the Island wasn't to be used for anything as silly as a high school yearbook. They exchanged addresses on small slips of paper, and used the inside of old envelopes to make notes.

Veronica wrote down several classmates' names and addresses on the inside of the envelope of the last letter she'd had from Mike. She smoothed the paper carefully, caressing it, as though she were touching Mike's face. "Someday," she spoke in a whisper to the soft warm day. "Someday soon."

Lana and Phillip talked for a long time. Veronica watched the two of them laughing and talking by the punch bowl. Then she saw Phillip reach over and pick a hibiscus flower and give it to Lana, who put it behind her ear.

Veronica sighed and turned her attention back to what Mrs. Nakamura and her mother were saying. She would miss Phillip's company and it was a bit deflating to see how quickly he'd been enchanted by Lana's charming smile. She'd once worried about Mike losing interest in her and falling for Lana.

Now it was Phillip who was leaving her. Life was funny.

Eventually, Phillip came back to escort her home, but she noticed that he didn't complain when she sent him home early. She kissed him on the cheek and said, "See you around."

"See you around," he answered. She watched as he walked down the driveway. His limp was almost gone now, and he walked like a happy man. She was happy for him. She stayed outside a long time, watching the sun go down and Hawaii sink into the darkness of the blackout.

Much later, her father came out and asked, "Smelling the flowers?"

"Not tonight."

"Where's Phillip?"

"I think he walked out of my life about an hour and a half ago," Veronica answered.

"That hurt?"

She slipped her arm through her father's and said, "Yes and no. It hurts to lose anyone, I guess. But I didn't want Phillip."

"And Mike will be home one of these days," her father said.

"Yes, he will." She had to believe that. She hadn't had a letter from him for almost a month and it was hard not to worry. But she was going to believe he would be back if it took all her courage and determination. And in the meantime, there was work to do.

"You and your mother really sound serious about this student nurse program."

"We are."

"One thing that's come out of this war," he said. "You and your mother. You're so much alike. I used to think you'd never be able to get along, but now you're a real team."

"I always thought I was like you," Veronica said.

"No. You're just like your mother," he said. "Pretty and sweet and intelligent." He kissed her cheek and then added, "And stubborn and independent and hardheaded."

"So you're going to let mother become a nurse," Veronica said. "I knew you would."

He hugged her briefly and said in a laughing voice, "I'm going to let you in on a little secret, Ronnie. I'm not going to *let* your mother do anything. You're mother has always done exactly what she wanted, and she's going to keep right on doing it."

"That's no secret," she teased him back. "I just didn't know you knew it."

"I'm leaving tomorrow," he said.

"Daddy, where you're going — is it dangerous?"

"It's all dangerous," he answered. "But I'll tell you this much, Ronnie. If where I'm going turns out all right, we'll know the war is ours."

"You mean we'll win?"

"Not overnight, but eventually. I promise you that."

There were three letters from Mike the next day, and they helped soften the sadness

of her father's departure. Mostly, Mike wrote about the things he missed from home, but she got the impression he was seeing quite a bit of action from one thing he said: "The Germans are tough fighters, Ronnie, but we'll win because we're right."

In Hawaii, rumors were flying that the Japanese were on their way to invade the Hawaiian Islands. On June 8th, the news was quite marvelous. A huge Japanese invasion force had been heading for the Hawaiian Islands but were headed off at Midway. Sailors, soldiers, and Marines all converged on the Japanese ships and fought a huge naval battle. The United States won. It was the first real victory of the war, and the people of Hawaii were jubilant.

Veronica went through the downtown section of Honolulu on her way to the hospital. It was in the middle of the day and people were so excited that they'd closed their shops and were in the streets. There was so much excitement and happiness in the air that she paused to watch the celebration.

There were people dancing in the streets. She saw Mike's Uncle Tu hugging and kissing a little old Chinese woman in black trousers. She saw storekeepers and waiters and shipyard workers all congratulating each other over the wonderful news. Once, she thought she saw Lana and Phillip walking hand in hand in the crowd, but it turned out to be another happy couple.

Veronica walked on alone. She didn't want

to be late for her work and she was celebrating in her own quiet way by feeling secure for the first time. The war would eventually be over and the men she loved would return to her. One of these days Mike and her father, and the thousands of other men who were fighting for their country, would come home again. Hawaii would tear the black paper from its windows, turn on the lights in celebration, and the world would sing again.

Someday they would win the war and life would return to normal. And normal life allowed enough time for growing up and learning to love. She knew that she'd done a lot of growing up in the last six months, and by the time Mike came home, she'd be ready to love him. She walked briskly toward the hospital, imagining what it would be like to run toward Mike and throw herself in his arms. She would be so glad to see him and she would love him so much. Forever and ever.

Coming next from Sunfire: NICOLE, who is a passenger aboard the *Titanic*, finds love only to face losing it when the ship begins to sink.